A desperate, late-night phone call. A girl in trouble. A man with a guilt-haunted heart.

Lightning flashes out over the Gulf. **Thunder** rolls down Panama City Beach.

Thousands of bikers have descended on the Miracle Strip for one of America's premiere biker rallies. There's **energy, excitement, electricity.**

The twenty-seven miles of silky, sugar-white sand and emerald green waters of the Gulf of Mexico along the World's Most Beautiful Beaches are teeming with hot bikes and even hotter babes. It's a party in paradise, but **a storm is blowing in**, its approach relentless, pitiless, menacing.

Amid the bikes and beer and bikinis, **crimes of unspeakable brutality** are being commited—one of which touches too close to home for former reporter and lost soul Merrick McKnight.

Adrift, Merrick wanders around at night—alone and lonely— seeking **an elusive woman**, searching for a way back from the brink. Now, chasing down a vicious killer like the lead of a once-in-a-career type exclusive, Merrick is living the story of his life— and that's just what it might cost him.

Between crashes of thunder, **a killer strikes**, and a young woman's life hangs in the balance. Merrick will do anything he can to keep from losing her again, but will that be enough?

THUNDER
BEACH

By Michael Lister

TYRUS
BOOKS

Published by

Tyrus Books

1213 N. Sherman Ave. #306

Madison, WI 53704

www.tyrusbooks.com

Printed in the United States of America.

15 14 13 12 11 10   1 2 3 4 5 6 7 8 9 10

ISBN 9781935562047 (paperback)

ISBN 9781935562054 (hardcover)

For

Fran Oppenheimer

Michael Connelly

And the entire McKnight Clan

Angels all

Thanks so much for . . .

Invaluable editorial care and insight and investment . . .

Pam, Alison, Amy

Publishing bliss . . .

Ben, Alison, Amy

Wild nights (I mean research) in P-City and on PCB . . .

Tony Buoni, Ben LeRoy, David Murray, Raven, Tristan, Skye
(some names have been changed—may it please the innocent
and the guilty alike)

Friendship, encouragement, and love as a verb . . .

Meleah, Micah, Travis, Harley, Pam, Mike, Judi, Aimee, Claude,
Ida, Fran Oppenheimer, Bette Powell, Linda Macbeth, Jenny
Jones, Cricket Freeman, Alafair Burke, Michael Connelly,
Emily Balazs, Dave Lloyd, Steve Wiggins, David Murray, David
Vest, Jan Waddy, Elam Stoltzfus, Karen Turner, Crook Stewart,
Tammy Woods, Tony Simmons, Lynn Wallace, Buddy Wilkes,
Terry Lewis, Liz Jameson, Jim Pascoe, Michael Koryta, Jason
Hedden, Anitra Mayhann, and Jamie Smith.

The neon-lit night is electric.

Heat lightning flashes out over the Gulf as thunder rolls down Thomas Drive.

It's a warm May night, the air thick and humid beneath a bank of gunmetal-gray clouds, hovering in the dark night sky, heavy from holding back the approaching storm.

It's three days before I'll go to the Bay County Medical Examiner's office to identify her remains, and I'm shocked to see her bikini-clad body on the cover of the official event magazine of Thunder Beach, the semi-annual biker rally in Panama City.

I've come in search of a woman.

It seems I've spent my entire life searching for something—something elusive, evanescent—something that usually involves a woman. Ironically, the woman I'm here to see is not the woman I'll spend the next few days frantically trying to find.

The woman I'm in search of now, is here with her weekend-biker husband—or is supposed to be, and I've come hoping to catch a glimpse of her, hoping for her to see me. When we haven't seen each other or spoken for a while, I look for ways to remind her of my existence, to reignite the passion and attraction that's so obvious when we're together, so fast to fade when we're apart. Together, the intensity is like an exploding star. Apart, the light wave from that star decays so rapidly, and at such a short distance from the high energy event, it makes me question whether it really ever existed at all.

I've never been in a relationship quite like this one—from its unlikely birth in a VIP booth at The Dollhouse to this fire and ice, intimates/acquaintances dance we're doing now—I've never been as strung out on someone in my entire life.

Thunder Beach began in 1999. Known then as "Bike & Beach Bash," it was born out of an annual gathering of riders from Macon, Georgia, who always came down and stayed at the Sandpiper Beacon Beach Resort.

Following the first rally, the Bay County Tourist Development Council got involved, hired promoters, and changed the name to Thunder Beach.

After the 2000 rally, Joe Biggs came on board as an investor and advisor, and in 2001 became sole owner.

In 2001, just two weeks after the terrorists attacks of 9/11, Thunder Beach held its first autumn rally. Since then, the event has been twice a year—a smaller gathering in the fall and the premiere rally in the spring.

Over the years, Thunder Beach has grown into one of the best, most biker-friendly, free rallies in the country, attracting tens of thousands of riders twice yearly to the place locals call the world's most beautiful beaches.

I start at Ms. Newby's.

Regan is as likely to be here as anywhere. Though there are what seem like an infinite number of Thunder Beach venues, Ms. Newby's is ground zero.

The parking lot is filled with vendor tents, bikes, and people—the last lined up to watch as other bikes ride in. Moving through the mass of bodies, often coming to a complete stop, it's impossible not to touch and bump and brush up against others. At first, I say, Excuse me, to everyone, but quickly realize it's not necessary.

Inching through the parking lot, I scan the crowd searching for her.

It takes me a while, but I finally make it inside the covered patio. Black-clad bikers surround the bar in the round, stand in small groups butted up to each other talking, and press toward the stage and the Southern Rock band, Flirting With Disaster, playing a 38 Special cover.

There are so many people jammed into the small area, and this joint is like so many others around here, I think the city must send the fire marshal on vacation during Thunder Beach.

The patio floor is wet from melted ice, spilt drinks, and a light rain tracked in from earlier in the evening.

I am not a biker, and I'm not dressed like one. I stand out like a straight-edge at a freak party, but no one seems to notice. Maybe it's too dark or too crowded, or they're having too much fun to give a fuck.

Unable to find her at Ms. Newby's—though that doesn't mean she's not here—I walk down and check out Spinaker, La Vela, then cross the street to Dysfunction Junction.

On my way back, I hear my friend Dave Lloyd singing from beneath the covered porch of Hammerhead Fred's, and stop in for a song or two.

Because he knows how much I like them, he does Sting's "Fragile," then pulls out his ukulele and does a haunting, beachy groove version of Jim Croce's "Operator," Scott Neese backing him up on steel drums.

I think of Regan as they play, and the songs make me happy and sad at the same time, filling me with a pain-tinged longing, both crushing and comforting.

Thanking them, I drop a twenty into the open guitar case on the floor in front of the stage.

As I'm leaving Fred's, I hear someone call my name.

—Merrick?

I turn to see Stacie Adams, standing there, napkin in hand, big, genuine smile on her plain, pretty, pale face.

Beneath blond hair and big blue eyes, her large lips are painted a too-bright red—particularly against the whiteness of her skin, but her smile is so radiant everything else about her fades into the background.

—Hey, I say, giving her a hug.

She smells just the same—soapy clean with a hint of flower-scented hand cream.

—How are you stranger?

—I'm good. How are you?

—Good. You know …

Over beneath the large lighted sign, a family poses their red-cheeked children next to the enormous plastic shark hanging from a hook by its tail.

—Still waiting for you to call me for our next date, she says.

—Sorry, I say. I've meant to call, but have just had so much going on.

It's one of the great mysteries of life—why do we instantly connect with some people, no matter how unlikely, and not others. On paper, Stacie and I should be a far better match than me and Regan, but the heart isn't influenced by socioeconomic factors the way the head is.

Stacie and I were set up by a couple we both know. We went on a couple dates about five months ago, the week prior to me meeting Regan.

Our first date had been nice enough, but we probably would've just had the one, except she really seemed to have a good time. With very little in common and no real affinity for one another, our date was a little on the bland side for me, but as a single second grade teacher, Stacie is a good, kind, giving person without a lot of fun in her life, so I took her out a few more times to try and provide her with some.

—Yeah, yeah, yeah, she says.

—It's true, I say, but I'll call you next week.

—Don't say it if you don't mean it.

—I do and I will.

—Who, now. I didn't ask you to marry me, she says, her enormous smile reappearing. Easy with all the I do's and I will's.

I give her my best courteous laugh.

—I don't need your sympathy, she says.

—Huh?

—That laugh. Lacked authenticity.

—Sorry. I'm just tired.

—Listen, she says, turning serious. If you do call—

—I will.

—If we do go out again.

— We will, I say, and I mean it.

—Let's—

—How's next Thursday, I ask, cutting her off.

—Sure. Okay. But let's do something you enjoy.

—Okay.

—I know I had a better time than you when we went out before. It's sweet of you to take me out again, but I'll have fun doing anything that doesn't involve finger paint and glitter, so pick something you enjoy and let's do that.

—It's a date, I say, hug her goodbye, and resume my search, eventually returning to Ms. Newby's where I began.

It's early and most places are still pretty quiet. Besides, it's Wednesday. The main action won't happen until the weekend.

This time, I enter the lounge/package store part of Ms. Newby's, and though just as crowded as the parking lot and patio, it's a lot cooler beneath the force of the frigid air blasting out of the vents.

Shuffling around the room, doing a kind of dance with the other patrons trying to move about, I search for her, looking mostly for her long, wavy, thick black hair—easily the best way to identify her in the throng.

So intense is my concentration for the raven-haired Regan that I bump into several people harder than I should, sloshing strong-smelling drinks onto our clothes and the floor, nearly walking directly in the path of a dart game in the process.

After a cup of Hunch Punch and almost an hour of looking for her, I give up in frustration and am about to leave when I see it.

It sits atop a stack of beer boxes, the official event magazine of Thunder Beach, and there's Casey—back arched, breasts out, hands reaching down to grab the strings of her bikini bottoms.

The old familiar guilt grips me, and I have a difficult time catching my breath.

I try to remember just how long it's been. Just over three years. She's changed so much in that time, transitioning from adolescent girl to young woman. I've spent so much time trying *not* to think about the whole situation—about Monica and Casey and Kevin and, most of all, little Ty—that I've only been vaguely aware of the expanding void at the center of my soul.

I've just come face to face with the single biggest regret of my life, and it rocks me, but I quickly realize what I'm witnessing isn't only a painful reminder, but a hope-inspiring opportunity. Casey is back. I've got to find her, to beg her forgiveness and make things right. Is it too late? Will she forgive me? Can I make it up to her?

Suddenly wet with sweat, room spinning, heart pounding, I can feel the Hunch Punch coming up.

Grabbing the glossy publication, I rush toward the bathroom and run directly into Regan.

—Merrick?

She looks distressed to see me, looks over my shoulder and all around us, then seems to grow even more distressed at how I look.

—You okay?

I shake my head.

—What is it?

I hold up the magazine.

Her eyes widen and she seems to recognize Casey, though I've never mentioned her.

—You recognize her? I ask.

—What're you doin' here? Are you following me?

—*No.*

—Then what?

—Looking for *her*, I say, nodding at the magazine cover. Technically, it's the truth now, but it still tastes like a lie on my tongue. Do you know her?

—Here comes Gabe, she says. I've got to go.

—You working later tonight? I ask, but she's moved on—something I need to do—and I don't get my answer.

I stumble into the restroom, splash some water on my face, and attempt to pull myself together.

What the fuck am I doing in a relationship with a married stripper?

What am I doing with a stripper at all?

Before I got to know Regan and some of the other girls she works with, I probably had some of the same stereotypical assumptions about strippers as the masses, but the dancers I know in general and Regan in particular, like most people, continually surprise and delight and shatter society's shallow caricatures of them.

When I come out of the restroom, Regan and Gabe are gone.

I wait in line for a turn at the bar. When I get it, I order something I don't intend to drink from a bartender who's far too busy for more than a perfunctory greeting.

—What can I getcha?

—You seen her around? I ask, plopping the magazine on the bar and pointing at Casey.

—They got a booth outside, he says, with barely a glance.

—Who?

—Eight bucks, he says, nodding toward the drink, then moves down to do refills.

—You Merrick McKnight? the guy on the stool to my left asks.

—Yeah?

—Used to read your column in the *Democrat*. Liked it—a lot. What happened to it?

—You read the online or print version? I ask.

—Computer.

—That's what happened.

—You were good.

—Still am, I say, but if a writer falls in the woods …

—I hear ya.

I drop a ten on the bar beside the untouched drink, and head outside.

It takes a while because of the crowd, but eventually I locate the Thunder Beach Productions booth sandwiched between a stall for Vintage Leather Enterprises biker apparel and one for collectable Case pocket knives.

Behind a table filled with stacks of various editions of the Thunder Beach Magazine, and in front of poster size prints of Miss Thunder Beach Contest models in bathing suits, two young guys with cups of Hunch Punch stand around eyeing the crowd.

—We'll have some more of the new one in a minute, one of the guys says.

—I'm looking for her, I say, pointing to Casey's picture on the cover of the magazine I'm holding.

—You and every other horny bastard on the beach, one of them says.

—Which one is that? the other one asks, leaning in to see.

—She's a little too young for you, don't you think? the first one adds.

—It's not like that. Where can I find her? It's important.

—We just pass out the magazines. Can't help you.

—The office number's in the front, the other one adds. Talk to somebody who knows something.

—It'd be refreshing, I say.

Beneath a streetlight next to Thomas Drive, I find the office number to Thunder Beach Productions and punch it into my phone.

As I expect, I get voicemail, and leave a message for the person listed as being the Miss Thunder Beach Program Manager.

I try to impart just how important it is that she call me back, that I talk to her cover girl, without sounding like a perv. Several times I have to stop talking and repeat myself because of the bikes thundering by on the street in front of me.

As I'm about to leave Ms. Newby's, I think I see Casey in the crowd at the side, not far from the patio.

I try to rush over, but the crowd prevents me from doing anything but edge along at a crawl.

When I finally arrive where I thought I saw her, she is gone.

I look around for a while, searching every face I encounter for the familiar, yet foreign face that feels like a blade being buried just below my ribcage—all the more because she looks like her mother now and makes me wonder what Ty would've looked like—but she's not here and probably never was.

It must have been a trick of light, the night, or my guilt-memory, and I wonder how many more times it will happen before I find her.

I'm almost to my car, when a thick, muscular black man steps from between two other vehicles and holds up a copy of the Thunder Beach Magazine.

—Heard you were lookin' for her.

The issue he's holding is different from the one I have. In it, Casey is wearing a different swimsuit.

—I asked you a question, he says.

Actually, he didn't, but I'm smart enough not to point that out.

His massive upper body, which looks perpetually flexed, presses against a too-tight light blue T-shirt, and the circumference of his neck is larger than my thigh.

I glance around, my heart rocking around my ribcage.

—It's just us, he says. Ain't gonna hurt you. Just got a message for you.

—Okay, I say stepping back a bit, trying to ease out of arm's reach from him.

—Whatever you heard, why ever you're lookin', don't. Just let it go. Move on. Always other girls.

I stare at him in stunned silence, wondering what Casey's involved in, wondering what I can do about it.

—Nod if you understand me, he says.

I must not have done anything because he says it again.

I nod.

—Let this be the end of it, my friend, he says, his voice light and jovial, as if he's just expressing genuine concern.

—Nod if you're gonna let this go.

I don't do anything.

—Do yourself a favor and nod your fuckin' head.

I hold his gaze, but don't move.

—A subsequent visit will not be so pleasant, he says, pressing the magazine into my chest as he walks off.

I drive by The Dollhouse, searching the lot for her car.

Most dancers park on the right side of the building beneath a couple of security lamps, a bouncer escorting them back to their cars when their shift ends.

Still shaken by the threat I'd received in the parking lot before leaving, I'm out of sorts, desperate to find Casey, to try and help her out of whatever fix she's in.

Regan's car isn't there.

I probably left the beach too soon. Crossing the Hathaway Bridge and coming back into town hadn't taken nearly as long as I thought it would. I could've stayed longer and kept looking for Casey, but Regan recognized her—maybe even knew of her connection to me—and since I was jonesing to see her anyway, why not get the information from her instead of cruising around PCB to events it's unlikely Casey would be at until the weekend anyway—if at all. Just because she's on the cover of the Thunder Beach Magazine doesn't mean she's actually going to be at Thunder Beach activities. And if she is, if there's a Miss Thunder Beach competition, it'd take place over the weekend.

Obviously Casey's in trouble, and though I'm not sure what I can do, I don't think it's just chance that I found out about it. I'm not saying it's fate—or that I even believe in such things. Life's too random to be fated, but I don't think it's a coincidence either. Whatever it is, now that I know, I'll do everything I can to help her—and not because I expect it to diminish the guilt I feel. I know nothing can do that. I'll help Casey because I must.

Not ready to go into the club yet—not going in at all if she's not working, I stay on 98, deciding to drive around and wait for her to arrive.

I like to drive—especially at night.

Earlier in the evening, with the sun a coral-colored glow on the brow of gathering clouds, I had left the tiny town where I live and driven west toward the ebbing light of the diminishing day.

My new car, and part of the reason I like to drive so much, is a retro, deep water blue Dodge Challenger

Victim of both a bad economy and an industry that was already gasping for breath back when things were good, I'm a former reporter—unemployed, untethered, unsure of my next step. So I wander around, mostly at night, in the car I bought a week before I lost my job.

Lost.

Alone.

Searching.

The Panhandle of Florida is dotted with a smattering of small towns. Racing down rural roads is a way of life.

I live in a town of a few thousand people, half an hour from Panama City, called Wewathitchka—Wewa to locals—where for four generations the McKnights, my family, owned and operated the weekly newspaper and produced tupelo honey (the self-employed in small towns rarely do just one thing). Breaking my dad's heart, I had taken a job with a corporate-owned wire service, working special assignments all over the Panhandle—from state government in Tallahassee to tourism in Panama City Beach and crime everywhere in between—until declining ad revenues at the dailys and the rise of free online news meant there wasn't a market for what I did.

At the moment, my sole source of income is two classes I teach at the college—one writing, one philosophy—and it isn't enough to cover my car payment.

I've thought about trying to revive my family's weekly, which Dad had been forced to close a year or so ago because of bad health and my absence, but even if I could make it work—which is doubtful—it'd be short lived. The days of newspapers, at least in their current form, are numbered. Soon, they will go the way of payphones and typewriters and literary magazines—there'll probably always be a few, but the age of their dominance has come to an end.

I ride around for a while, mostly through St. Andrews, past the Shrimp Boat, Tan Fanny's, Uncle Earnie's, then park and walk around the marina and Oaks by the Bay. The fresh air and the walk do me good, giving me some much needed perspective, even peace, and by the time I arrive back at The Dollhouse and see Regan's car, I'm in a better place.

As I park near her car and kill the engine, my phone vibrates in my pocket.

—Hello.

—This Mr. McKnight?

The female voice is professional, but tired and not happy to be making the call.

—Yeah?

—You called about Miss Thunder Beach.

—Yes. I'm looking for Casey. She's—

—Sir, we can't give out any information about our contestants, but—

—But I'm … family.

—Then you'll know how to contact her.

—We lost touch, I say, realizing how ridiculous it sounds. I'm not a fan or a stalker. I'm her … I was her—

—Sorry I can't help you.

—Could you give her my number? You could do that, couldn't you? I think she may be in trouble.

—If you really believe that you should report it to the police. Otherwise, I don't know what else to tell you. All the contestants will be appearing at various events this weekend, but we have very good security, so if you're coming to harass her in any way, you'll be removed—maybe even go to jail.

Energy.

Excitement.

Music vibrates the double entry doors.

Beyond the line of taxis, the front lot is reserved for bikes this week. There are fewer than I expect.

As usual, The Dollhouse is cold—management's way of keeping things fresh, frisky, and perky, and if it causes the dancers to huddle together in faux-lesbian fantasies when not performing or hustling, well, that's just an added bonus.

Smoke and mirrors.

The dim, mirrored room is loud and crowded, dance and disco lights piercing the smoke like airport lights through fog.

I show my ID and pay my cover, the bouncer looking from my flashlight-lit license up at me in recognition.

—You're here almost as much as me, he says.

I laugh, though the crack bothers me—as it had the first several times he used it on me.

Truth is, I only come about twice a month, but one week, during one of my more desperate times of missing Regan, I had come three times. The first two nights she was off, thus the repeat visits.

—Coming up next, we've got Raven on the main stage, the DJ announces over the dance remix of a recent hit, and Mystic in the play pen. Raven on the main and Mystic in the pen.

Just in time, I think.

Regan's stage name is Raven, owing to the hair, and I've arrived just in time to see her dance and tip her for her trouble. Most dancers only come over to customers who tip them while they're on stage, and though she'd come to see me anyway, it's good to follow protocol since we're trying to keep our relationship as secretive as what goes on in the VIP.

I find an empty table in the back corner, not far from the main stage, and scan the room.

The crowd is a good mix of male and female, young and old, bikers and regulars. Of course there are more men than women, but not by as much as most people would think.

The bar running along the left wall is full of patrons and dancers. In front of it, three guys surround the playpen—a small square stage with bars around it—waiting to tip the dancer.

I'm on the front side of the main stage, next to the hidden DJ booth. To my left, twenty or so customers sit at a handful of small tables. Behind us, there's a steady stream of people going to buy cigarettes, hit up the ATM machine, or into the bathroom to clean up from a dance or expel some cheap liquor. In front of us, a dancer named Diamond is finishing her set surrounded by two guys on each side of the stage.

Within the L made by the playpen and the main stage, the larger part of the room holds some twenty tables—over half-full so far tonight.

Beyond them a big bouncer with a clipboard stands at the entrance to the VIP rooms.

A waitress in tight black shorts, faux tuxedo top, and tennis shoes comes over to my table.

—What can I get you?

—Corona and a vodka and cranberry.

She smiles and nods, knowing that I've ordered for Raven.

As she leaves, I glance to my right, and in the small area between the DJ booth and the dressing room, I think I glimpse Casey again. In the fraction of a moment—there, blink, black, gone—the image dissolving into the dark hallway like a final frame of film fading to black.

The song ends or is faded—most are faded at the three-minute mark because some girl somewhere is always giving a lap dance—and Diamond squats down and gathers up her dollars, her large, natural boobs flopping around as she does.

—Okay fellas, we're setting those two lovely ladies lose and bringing up two more. If you want something more intimate, more private, the two ladies stepping down would love to take you back to VIP. Now, it's Mystic in the playpen and Raven on the main.

The music comes up and Raven, in a black teddy, climbs the stairs, hangs her small purse on the rail, wipes the pole with a cotton cloth towel, and begins her routine.

She is tall and trim and tan, her fuck-me pumps adding several inches, lifting her ass, and showing the muscles in her legs. The tiny black outfit emphasizes her hair and the overall darkness that is her—her deep, dark eyes and the brows that arch above them.

She is stunning, and I have to remind myself to breathe.

I grab some bills from my pocket and approach the stage.

Every dancer does a three song set—the first clothed, the second topless, the third with only a T-back or G-string. Almost nobody steps up to the tip rail before the girls bring their tits out, so I always make it a point to.

I stand at the stage, money folded long ways in hand, gazing up at her.

When she sees me, she smiles, and what appears to be genuine warmth brings her eyes to life as she drops to her knees in front of me.

—*He-ey*, she says.

—Hey.

—I'm glad you came in.

—You look amazing, I say. So beautiful.

—Thank you, sweetheart.

That stings a bit. She calls everyone sweetheart, and it sounds insincere in her mouth.

Whipping her hair around, she brushes it across my head and chest, then placing her hands on her black bra, she slowly shakes her cleavage in my face.

I know she has to, but I don't care for the standard stripper moves—not from her, not after what we've shared, but regardless of all that's gone before, tonight she's a stripper and I'm a customer.

When she finishes her customer routine, which includes sitting on the stage, open legs spread around me, arching her back, touching her breasts and rubbing her fingers across her crotch teasingly, she pulls back the string of her T-back and I slide the bills beneath it.

—Thank you, I say, and make my way back to my seat.

The waitress is waiting for me. She places the drinks on the table, I pay and tip her, and she's gone.

And I'm alone.

I'm leading a mostly solitary life these days, and mostly I don't mind it, but sitting alone in a strip club is sad—at least that's how most people view it. Pathetic old men, scary, anti-social young men—that's who sits alone at a strip club, and though I'm neither, doesn't change the perception.

I look like a regular being led around by his dick, but things are different with Regan—something every regular thinks about his girl. Like a shrink and her patients, the intimacy of sexual surrogacy that occurs between a stripper and her customer, causes the patient/customer to believe the relationship is somehow personal. And of course, it's to a stripper's benefit to make her clients believe that it is.

Only a fool falls in love with a stripper.

Every night strip clubs all over the world are full of fools.

I recall a conversation I had with Carl, a reporter friend, shortly after all this started.

—Remember what we were giving Greg shit about a few weeks ago? I ask.

—No.

—You don't?

—We give him shit all the time, he says. How'm I supposed to know what shit you're talking about?

—After we went to The Dollhouse.

—That he drinks too much? Can't hold his liquor? Throws all his money away at the first sign of titties?

—No.

—Then what? he asks. Shit. That's a lot of shit. We should probably lighten up on ol' Greg.

—What was the dumbest thing he did that night? I ask.

—Asked that fat stripper how much she weighed?

Carl has red hair and a pale, pudgy, freckle-flecked face, which reddens as he laughs at Greg's stupidity.

—No.

—Just tell me, he says.

—Fell in love.

—Oh. Well. That was dumb. But the dumbest thing he did was think that stripper—what was her name?

—Skye.

—Yeah. Skye. He went full retard when he thought *she* had fallen in love with *him*. That's what you meant? Why?

—I went and did the same thing, I say, frowning sheepishly. But it's different, I'm quick to add.

—Always is. 'Cept it ain't.

—Look at me, I say. It is. She fell for me first. I wasn't looking for anything, hadn't even crossed my mind.

—She fell for you first? Are you hearing yourself? They all make you think they've fallen for you. That's what they do.

—You don't think I know that? Don't think I had my guard up against the game? This is different. It is. I'm telling you.

Carl shakes his head.

—Yes you are, he says.

—What?

—Telling me. Over and over. You know how many time's you've told me how different it is?

—Okay, I say, tell me this. Why do they pretend to like customers?

—For bank.

—Exactly.

—And?

—We've been together three months.

—Been together? Are you serious? I can't believe you—Let me ask you this?

—Okay.

—She been to your mama's house yet?

—Not yet, I say, but she will. And she hasn't asked me for anything.

—What?

—She's not using me. She's not. There's no hustle.

—Yet. The best hustles are the ones that seem like there's no hustle.

Maybe Carl is right. Maybe the hustle is coming, but I don't think so.

What I have with Regan is different. I'm different than most of The Dollhouse patrons, and she's different than most of The Dollhouse dancers. At least this is what I keep telling myself—like the mindless mantra of the immature and insecure.

And I really believe it—particularly when I'm with her.

As I often do, I think back to how it began.

It started with a kiss.

I had come to The Dollhouse for a bachelor party. It was the second one in a month, and remembering her from the first, I was hoping to see her again.

It was only my second time at The Dollhouse, and though I wasn't close with the old college friends, I was having a blast.

The best man paid for each of us to have a lap dance with the girl of our choice. We could have it at our seat or pony up the extra ten bucks to rent the VIP for half an hour. We could even get additional dances for twenty a pop if we were of a mind.

I chose Raven and kicked in the extra Hamilton for the privacy.

This was my third lap dance, so I knew how to act and what to expect. Though what you could do varied from club to club, I was always a submissive, hands-at-my-sides, perfect gentleman.

And then she kissed me.

—You're so handsome, she says. So hot. I was attracted to you from the moment you first walked in.

I recall how she came up to me the first time we saw each other in the club and how when I told her she was so beautiful, she told me I was handsome, how it had seemed so sincere, how she hadn't told any of the other guys that, how there was a spark, a connection from the very beginning—or so it seemed—but I knew she was working. It was her job to be nice to everyone, to flirt, to be what the customers wanted her to be. But everything she did seemed so genuine. There was a light in her eyes, a goodness that emanated from her. We seemed to have something real, and I would've liked to talk to her more, but the groom-to-be wanted her attention, so I didn't think anything else about it.

—Put your hands on me, she says. I want you to touch me.

Her eyes lock on mine as she dances on my body, and though I know all the best strippers make serious eye contact, this seems different. I am mesmerized.

My body responds to hers—but not just my body, all of me.

Her long, thick, black hair is like a beaded curtain around us, her perfectly shaped breasts pressing against me, our tongues darting in and out of each other's mouths.

It was so intense, so genuine, so unexpected—and all the more incredible for it.

When our time was up, when she was dressed again, she had said,

Please don't tell your friend. I didn't do that with him. I've never done that with anyone.

I want to believe her and actually do, but decide to enjoy it for what it is—even if I'm not the only customer she's done such things with.

I left that night high on her, grateful for such a rare and unique experience, hoping to see her again someday, but not expecting to. Not really—even though we had exchanged numbers. Then, she called and we began to talk and text, and what started off with a kiss had grown into an obsession.

We meet the next week over hot chocolate and talk about what happened. She is shy and embarrassed, but honest, and we bond.

I leave the all-night omelet shop with no expectations, but she calls a little while later and asks to meet the following week when she returns to town.

I'm delighted and look forward to it, and though she is held up and has to cancel, our relationship begins in earnest, in spite of how often she has to break our dates.

She finishes up her three song set, collects her money, dresses, and makes her rounds to thank her tippers, rewarding each with a hug or quick kiss on the cheek.

As I had hoped, she saves me for last, joining me at the small table.

—This for me? she asks, nodding toward the drink.

I frown.

—Of course. Probably a little watery by now. They got it out faster than I thought they would.

—Thanks.

She stirs the vodka and cranberry around, then drops the stirrer on the table, lifts and drinks about a third of it.

—I'm glad you came in. How are you?

She says the same things over and over in here—at least at first—but so do I.

—Good, I say, which I always do whether I am or not. How are you?

—Little tired, but good. Happy to see you.

—Really?

She gives me a wide-eyed smirk.

—Of course.

I let it go.

—How was Thunder Beach? I ask.

She shrugs.

—More Gabe's thing, but it was okay. Scared hell out of me when I saw you.

—Sorry.

—I don't want to hurt him. I can't. He's too …

She doesn't finish. She doesn't have to. I know she means fragile or vulnerable, but I also know she'd never use those words to describe her disintegrating, out-of-work husband.

I feel a pang of guilt, as I always do when I think about her husband. I've never met the man—what I know of him, I know only through her—and though their relationship is dead, it hasn't been buried yet, and I know I should wait until it is to get involved with her, but selfishly, recklessly, I have not. To justify what we're doing, we've set boundaries, lines we haven't and won't cross, but I know what we're doing is wrong—mostly because of the deception and dishonesty involved.

I'm anxious to ask her about Casey, but don't want to do anything to jeopardize the little time we have together, so decide to ask her toward the end of our interaction.

—Were you following me? she asks.

—*No*, I say with conviction, because it's true. Looking for and following are two different things.

—What were you doing out there?

—Looking for Casey, I say, which is what I ended up doing, though not what I went out there to do.

She looks away, pretending to be distracted by what another dancer is doing on stage.

We finish our drinks, and I want to ask her for some private time in the back, but, as always, am a bit apprehensive. Why? I wonder. Is it fear of rejection? She's a sure thing. It's her job. But I'm wanting it to be more than a job, more than just what she'd do for any man with money.

The DJ announces it's time for two-for-one, and she rolls her eyes and frowns.

—I hate these, she says.

—Is it too late for us to go to VIP so you won't have to do it?

She shakes her head.

I pull a ten out of my pocket and lay it on the table in front of her.

—I'll be right back, she says, and walks over to the reception area.

During the two-for-one, all the dancers not in VIP line up, walk across the main stage either wearing a special Dollhouse T-shirt or carrying a shot, then scatter into the audience to offer patrons two dances for the price of one, plus either the shirt or shot. The dances are performed right at the customer's chair, saving the charge for the private room.

I've never met a dancer who didn't hate the two-for-ones, and that goes double for Raven. It makes her feel even more like a piece of meat on display than usual, and is followed by a long line of rejections, and possibly something worse. If during the first song, the dancers can't find a taker for the special offer, they have to climb back on the stage and dance together for the next two songs in what they refer to as the "losers" dance.

Raven returns with a slip for the DJ, and I wait while she takes it to him. It lets him know to keep her out of the rotation for the next half-hour, but also when to announce that the thirty minutes is over by saying—Raven, check's out. Raven, check's out.

Once she returns from the DJ booth, she takes me by the hand, like every other VIP customer, and begins to lead me toward the back.

When we're about halfway, a tall, skinny, young dancer with multiple piercings jumps up from a table, slaps a patron, then yells for the bouncer. Before the bouncer can get there, the patron gets up, grabs the girl, lifts her, and body slams her onto the ground.

The bouncer is there by then, grabbing the guy, only to have the guy's two friends join in.

I pull Regan back and stand between her and the fight.

The bouncer is a huge black man and the three guys are drunk as fuck, but three against one—even three drunks—isn't fair, and I wonder if I should help. Just then another bouncer runs past us and joins in. Within a few seconds, the fight is over, the men subdued, the police called.

Raven and I continue to VIP.

Without the bouncer at the door, we get our choice of rooms, and she leads me to the one at the end that has no camera in it, the one we lucked into the first night we were together.

—This is my favorite room, I say.

She smiles.

Each VIP suite is a four-by-four booth with a small built-in couch on one side and a mirror on the other. The entry of each is a beaded curtain, which like the carpet and the fabric on the couch has images of strippers painted on it.

I'm vaguely aware we're in a VIP room at The Dollhouse, but we could be anywhere in the world. It feels like we're the only two people on the planet. The bouncer just beyond the beads, the others—dancers and shooter girls, regulars and first-timers—have all faded so far into the background they no longer exist. Everything has faded, everything.

—What're you thinking? she asks, as she always does when we're back here.

—About this. Us. It still doesn't seem real. I didn't come in here looking for … well, anything.

—I know you didn't. I certainly don't come to work looking for a …

She doesn't seem to know what to call me.

Her top is off. Her thick, long, dark hair frames her sweet beautiful face and falls down to cover her breasts so that she looks like a chaste painting of Eve in the Garden of Eden.

How apropos, I think, an image associated with forbidden fruit.

The song changes and outside the curtain, the tall white bouncer passes by with his clipboard, marking which girls are giving dances so the house is sure to get its cut.

We both look at the mirror across from us.

She looks like a ballerina, and I want to see her dance in other ways, on other stages.

Even seated, the C-section scar, like a smile on her lower abdomen, is visible.

The first time she had pointed it out, I had called it the smile of motherhood, but that had been before I knew, before we had bonded over loss only people in our position could understand. Now, I just trace it with the tip of my finger.

I'm trying to think of the best way to ask her about Casey when she stands and says—You ready?

I nod, though I'd really rather continue doing what we're doing.

—Slide over, she says, and spread 'em.

I do as I am told, moving to the center of the small couch and spreading my legs.

A new song comes on, and she begins to dance for me. I'm instantly erect.

—Put your hands on me, she says.

I do.

We've yet to make love, though we've done nearly everything but. The time we came close, I was getting ready to enter her after a half-hour of intense foreplay, when she said, There's still a line we haven't crossed, and I stopped.

Always far more forward and amorous when we're here in VIP than when we're by ourselves, she explained that she knows she can only go so far in here, where as when we're alone together outside of this place, she knows she's unlikely to stop.

—I want to feel you, she says.

My hands are on her lovely, soft breasts, my mouth on her large protruding nipples—like the scar, one of the few signs she had once been a mother.

—Can I feel you? she asks.

I nod.

She shifts, placing herself just above the erection bulging beneath my jeans, and begins to thrust.

—God, you make me so hot, she says. I've never been this physically attracted to anyone.

I appreciate the compliment, but wonder at the qualification. Is this just physical for her?

As she continues to rub herself on me, as we continue to kiss and I caress her, her state of arousal intensifies, and it turns me on all the more.

—Can I? she asks.

—Please, I say, not exactly sure what's she's talking about, but hoping it's what I think it is.

She grabs me and straightens me up inside my jeans, then begins to rub more rapidly, her breathing and moans growing.

I hold her tight, gripped by far more than desire, and I realize I love her.

She continues until she comes, and as she does, I lift my hand up and cup the side of her face beneath her raven hair and hold her close.

Oh my God, she says breathlessly. That was amazing.

—You're amazing, I say.

—Thank you so much. I owe *you* for that one. Or owe you one of those.

She is the most sexual, most sensuous woman I've ever been with, and I love that about her. I desire her more than I've ever desired anyone else, but her owing me an orgasm or even having one myself has not even crossed my mind—so caught up am I in her experience.

—I keep doing things with you that I've never done with anyone, she says.

I squeeze her tighter.

—I don't want to, but I have to move, she says. I can't be touching you when I'm not dancing.

We uncurl from each other, and she slides over to sit beside me.

Her hair falls down to cover her breasts like before, as she tucks her feet beneath her. Reaching over, she takes my hand, lacing our fingers like we might if we were in high school.

We are quiet a long moment.

Knowing our time is growing short, I realize I need to talk to her about Casey, but hate to so close to such an intensely intimate moment. I'm trying to come up with a good way to broach the subject, when I hear the DJ.

—Raven, check's out. Raven, check's out.

—You recognized the girl on the Thunder Beach Magazine, I say.

—I've got to go, she says, standing, slipping back into her clothes.

—How do you know her, I say, getting up, too, and pulling out my wallet.

—Just pay me for one, she says. I really should be paying you.

She always tells me to just pay for one dance, which keeps her from losing money to the house, but I nearly always give her more.

—I don't think I know her, she says. I guess I thought I knew who you were talking about.

—What does that mean?

—Doesn't matter.

—Do you know Casey?

—I don't really want to get in the middle of this. Please just let me—

—How do you know her?

—Let me give her a message for you. I can do that. If she wants to contact you, she will.

—She doesn't work here, does she?

I can tell by her face that she does.

My little Casey working as a stripper. How can this be?

—Why haven't I ever seen her?

—Because, she says, she hides in the dressing room when you're here.

—She does?

—She didn't want you to know she's dancing. Please just let me give her your number. I'm sure she'll call you. What's the story between you two?

—She didn't tell you?

She shakes her head.

—Why didn't you tell me? I ask.

—It wasn't my place. Really. I couldn't—

—Raven, check's out. Raven.

—I've got to go, she says. I'm gonna get in trouble.

—Give her my number, I say. Tell her I'm sorry for everything. I didn't know she was living here again. I'd love to see her and catch up. I'd love to do anything I can for her.

—I'll tell her.

—Can I see you tomorrow?

—I'll call you.

—I love you, I say as she's rushing away, and though I know she heard me, she doesn't respond.

I'm barely out of the parking lot, carefully maneuvering around packs of bikes on 98, when she calls.

—Hey, she says.

I recognize her voice immediately, though it's been quite a while since I've heard it.

Unbidden, a random memory of Casey unfolds in my mind. It's

the night of the middle school winter ball. In limbo, torn between girl child and pubescent princess, she is radiant in a ruby dress and black patent leather shoes, elaborate up do, blonde ringlets cascading down around an innocent face touched for the first time with a light dusting of makeup. When I remove the corsage I've gotten her from the green tissue, her eyes light up with genuine joy and gratitude.

—Hey, Case. Thanks for calling. It's so good to hear from you. When'd you move back to Panama City?

I hear the DJ in the background as a door opens.

—I've got to go. They're about to call me on stage.

Lightning continues to flicker in the distance, random drops of rain falling here and there, but it appears as though the storm will hold off for now.

—Can we meet when you get off? Get some coffee or something.

—It's not until four.

—I know. We can get breakfast if you like.

—Sure. Okay. Meet you at Coram's at four-thirty.

—Which one?

—Huh?

—Which Coram's?

—Beach, she says. Thomas Drive.

—I'll be there.

Looking at the time on my phone, I realize I've got just a little under four hours to kill. I think about it for a few moments and decide on three different things. First, I'll swing by Player's, where two of my students are competing in a poker tournament for a seat at the World Series of Poker, then I'll stop by Joe's for some wings, then I'll hang out at The Curve where a friend of mine is spinning records.

Since I'm already driving west on 98, I continue to the college and turn onto 23rd, heading back east toward town.

Though the rally doesn't kick it up into overdrive until closer to the weekend, there are still a lot more bikes on the street than usual, their diversity staggering.

In the lane next to me, a young guy in beach attire on a black American Ironhorse Slammer with red and yellow designs, chrome v-handle bars, wheels, and sidewinder engine rides beside an older woman in faded denim and bandanas on an electric-blue Harley Road King Classic with leather bags and whitewall tires, a large American flag mounted on the back of her bike rippling in the wind of her wake.

Player's is a sports club on 23rd Street with 8,000 square feet of gaming—from eleven regulation billiards tables to electronic dartboards to ping pong. Some nights there's karaoke or a DJ, others there's billiards or darts tournaments, but tonight, it's poker.

I sit at the bar and order a glass of red wine and wait for Stephen and Kyle to get a break. Beyond the bar, at some twenty tables, amateur poker players are holding and raising and calling and winning and losing.

Unlike other nights, Player's is quiet. With no music to disturb the tournament, nothing else going on in the place, and the concentrated hush over the crowd, it sounds more like a cafeteria than a sports bar.

This is the second of two tournaments tonight, and has fewer players. In the time it takes me to sip my way through the glass of wine, a steady stream of people stand, dejected, and walk away from their table, either to the bar for a consolation drink or out of the club, merely grunting their goodbyes if someone speaks to them.

After about thirty minutes, a break is announced, and Kyle and Stephen make their way over to me at the bar.

—What's up *prof-es-sor*? Stephen, the more outgoing of the two, says.

—Teach, Kyle adds.

They are both in their early twenties, with long, unruly hair flowing from beneath baseball caps. Stephen is trim and wears a trendy American Eagle shorts and shirt set. Kyle's six-six, two-sixty muscular frame is always covered in what he can find to fit it—usually jeans and a T-shirt.

—How's it looking? I ask. Either one of you gonna be headin' to Vegas?

—I'm doin' okay, Stephen says. The chip leader at my table, but the cards I'm gettin' are for shit.

—I'll be out this next round, Kyle says.

—Whatta you up to tonight? Stephen asks.

—Hanging, I say. Hittin' up a little bit of Thunder Beach.

—Cool. We're gonna go out after this if you wanna hang around. Probably the Toy Box or Spinaker.

—Got a friend spinning 80s music at The Curve, I say, but I appreciate it.

—Maybe we'll swing by.

As I climb into my car, my phone rings.

In the moment before I look at the display, I hope it's Regan. I have the same reaction every time it rings these days.

I don't recognize the number, and I wonder, as I always do, if it's Regan's husband, Gabe. Rarely do calls this late bring good news.

I know it's not Casey because I programmed her number in after she called, and her name would appear on the screen.

I take a breath and press the answer button.

—Hello.

—You the one lookin' for Miss Thunder Beach? Want something extra special?

The harsh, gravely voice vibrates up through cigarette burned vocal chords. It's aggressive, menacing, and though age and race are difficult to discern, I picture a large, mean white man in his mid to late fifties who's spent a lot of time around black guys.

—Yeah, but I found her.

—What? You what?

—I found her.

—The fuck you mean *you found her*?

—Who is this? I ask.

—The fuck is this?

—Stay away from her, I say, but it doesn't come out as threatening as I'd like.

He ends the call, and when I call the number back it goes directly to a voicemail box with no personal greeting, just the generic, computerized one that gives the number, but no name.

The call unnerves me, and I wonder again what Casey's gotten herself mixed up in.

Joe's Corner Pub, on 98 not far from the college, is a small joint that according to its sign serves the best hot wings in town.

Dark, loud, smoky, and devoid of tourists, Joe's is everything a local's pub should be.

I sit at the bar beneath '70s-style hanging stained glass Busch and Michelob lamps and look around.

Behind me, at one of two pool tables beneath black Bud Light lamps, two emaciated men in shorts, flip flops, soiled shirts and caps attempt to shoot pool though they can barely stand up.

—Gotta dollar?

I turn to see a thin, middle-aged woman with a ponytail holding up two dollars.

—Huh?

—For the jukebox, she says. Got a dollar for the jukebox.

—Sure, I say, looking over at the internet jukebox on the far wall between the two flat screens playing sports programs.

I dig out a dollar and hand it to her.

—Got a request? she asks, but doesn't wait for my response.

Surprisingly, Joe's is busy, the bar nearly full, and the lone bartender rushes past me, cigarette in one hand, beer in another, serving the late night patrons.

—What can I get you?

—Tecate and a dozen wings, I say. Hot with ranch.

—Don't have Tecate.

—Corona?

She nods and is gone, disappearing beneath the blue neon Joe's Corner Pub sign and into the small kitchen. Bartenders at Joe's also cook the wings.

There are a few bikers in town for the rally scattered throughout the joint, but only a few. This is a locals' place—one you have to look for to find.

—Lime? the bartender asks, placing my Corona on a green Rolling Rock coaster.

—Please.

She shoves a small slice of lime all the way down into my beer and is off again.

—Merrick McKnight, a slurring female voice says.

I turn to see April Jen trying to climb onto the stool next to me.

—Hey April, I say, and help her onto the stool.

A true alcoholic, I've never encountered April—no matter the time, day or night—when she didn't smell like alcohol and seem under its influence. A few years ahead of me in high school, April's family owned the package store in Wewa, and I had always felt sorry for her. Back then, I made a point of speaking to her, sitting next to her if she were alone in the lunchroom or gym or on the bus.

—How the hell are you? she asks, leaning in unsteadily—too close, too familiar.

—I'm okay. How are you?

—What the hell you doin' here? she asks. I've never seen you here before. Is this your kind of place? I wouldn't think this is your kind of place.

—I love it here. Came to get some wings, I say. Missed supper.

—Carol, she shouts. Carol.

A brunette with family resemblance staggers over to us from further down the bar.

—This is Merrick. Guy I told you 'bout. Nicest guy in Gulf County. This is Carol, my cousin.

—He's all hawt too, Carol says. You are. Look at that cute face and hard body.

—Thanks, cousin Carol, I say.

Of course, it's too dark to see much of anything in the bar, and she's too drunk to see much of anything even if it weren't.

The metallic *chook-chook* of coins sliding and the ceramic *pop* of the balls dropping is followed a moment later by the *crack* of the break—and a new game of pool is begun.

April and Carol continue to talk, and I just toss in an occasional uh-huh, really, or nod.

My wings arrive, and though I had asked for ranch, the blue cheese on the plate is homemade and so good I don't correct the mistake. The wings are small and crispy and hot and live up to the advertisement as the best in town. I should know. I've tried them all.

—Either of you ladies care for a wing? I ask.

—I'm on a liquid diet, April says.

Carol laughs like it's the funniest thing she's ever heard.

I eat my wings and drink my beer faster than I normally would, yet still enjoying every bite, and though I'm tempted to order another dozen, resist the urge and head back out to the beach.

Driving past the college, the port of Panama City, and over the Hathaway Bridge in a light drizzle, I listen to a club mix put together by Miguel on Island 106, bouncing to the beat, feeling the pulse of the night, seeing the million lights of the beach through a smattering of raindrops on my windshield.

The storm's coming—I can feel it in the atmosphere, but so far it's only a threat—looming, impending, inevitable.

The Hathaway Bridge connects two worlds—one of dreams, of paradisiacal fantasies, of concrete condos, giant houses built on sand; the other, of small town sensibilities, deep South traditions, of paper mill and port and public Protestantism.

Arriving out at the beach with even more time to kill than I planned, I remember Steve Wiggins is hosting jam night in the piano bar of The Grand Towers, and stop by before heading to The Curve.

Every Wednesday night, Steve Wiggins, great guy and amazing musician, invites anyone who'd like, to bring an instrument and sit in on the best, most eclectic jam session on the beach.

The music is good, but what I like most is the atmosphere. Everyone is welcomed and encouraged—no matter their skill level.

In a living room like environment, we sit on sofas and chairs in front of a flickering faux fireplace and sip spirits to the soothing sounds of mostly blues standards.

Just before I leave, Lenwood Cherry sits down at the drums, Kerry McNeil takes up the bass, and with Steve on piano, they perform a blues version of "Ain't No Sunshine" with Lenwood taking care of vocals. Lenwood's voice is soulful and resonant and nearly as smooth as his touch on the drums.

I find Tristan in the parking lot of The Curve, having a smoke with Brad, the bouncer. Located on the curve of Thomas Drive, the place is actually called Ms. Newby's Too, but just as often goes by The Curve.

Bikes are lined up across the front of the building, cars and trucks further back in the lot. Next to the door, beneath a small tent, Sweet Racks is selling what many locals argue is the barbeque equivalent of a multiple orgasm.

—Ciao baby, Tristan says, giving me his standard greeting.

A couple of years my junior, he's a thin, dark, much inked, much pierced, punk rocker in all black. His black eyes are made more so by the eyeliner around them, which matches the paint on his nails. In contrast to all the black and the dark, brooding vibe emanating from him, his short, spiky hair is a shock of peroxide white-blond.

—'Sup Merrick, Brad adds.

Average size, Brad is small for a bouncer, but he's a badass motherfucker, and nobody messes with him more than once.

—How's tricks, fellas?

—Brad to the bone just fucked up some poor poser, Tristan says.

—Punk ass bitch drives down here in his Cadillac pulling his bike in a twenty-thousand dollar trailer then wants to act like he's pimp and push people around. Shee-it. Not on my watch.

—Where is he?

—Ambulance just carried him to the hospital, Tristan says.

—Really?

—I shit you not.

Brad runs a hand over his shaved head, absently rubbing the voodoo skeleton death mask on the side of his skull.

—Time to get back to work, Tristan says. Those records won't spin themselves. Ciao.

Inside, Mai-Tai in hand, I stand on the stage in the backroom watching Tristan spin his magic.

Using two turntables, two CD players, and two iPods, Tristan presents a wicked mix of 80s music—much of it from the underground, club scene, or independent labels. Behind him on the wall, a large flat screen shows a series of images and video clips, live-action and animation, all from the '80s, which he compiled and edited to go with his set.

For the most part, the audience, largely comprised of bikers, doesn't appreciate the music, but when he throws in a dance version of an '80s hit, they fill the floor.

Quickly becoming my favorite drink, the Mai-Tai at The Curve is the most potent I've ever encountered. A mix of light and dark rums, orgeat syrup, Curacao, orange and lime juices, legend has it the drink was created by Victor Bergeron, the original owner of Trader Vic's.

According to him, he created it for a couple of Tahitian friends, who, upon tasting it, exclaimed, "Mai Tai," which means "out of this world."

I arrive at Coram's over a half-hour early, so anxious am I to see Casey.

The lot is empty save for one other vehicle, an electric-blue Chevy truck with monster tires and a long antenna, like a warped cane fishing pole, on the back.

Next to the front door, a woman in a red Coram's T-shirt and black apron leans on a *News Herald* box smoking a cigarette.

—One of the girls'll be right with you, she says, as I pass.

—No rush. I'm waiting on someone.

Like most waffle and omelet shops, Coram's kitchen runs along the back wall, fronted by a counter in the center and booths on either side, a tile floor aisle, with more tables and booths next to the plate glass windows along the front.

The color scheme is light beige and chocolate-brown, including the sand-colored tile of the floor—all of which sits beneath rows of bright florescent lights, making the place look like early morning even in the middle of the night.

I take a right and head toward the restroom, passing a youngish couple shoving in breakfast food, as I do.

Standing at the urinal, expelling the red wine, Corona, and Mai-Tai, I glance around and see someone has carved I'M IN LOVE into the red painted wood of the single stall.

Me, too, I think, and understand the compulsion to declare it in a public space—even the wall of a stall in a local diner restroom.

I'm in love with a stripper, I think. A married one at that. I admitted it to her tonight and only got silence.

Only fools fall for strippers, I can hear Carl saying.

I walk back into the dining area, past the couple, past the counter where one of the workers is now seated eating the Coram's special—heavenly hash with a side of blueberry muffin—to a booth on the far end, and sit facing the door.

A middle-aged waitress in a blue Coram's T-shirt, her hair in a ponytail, comes over with her pad.

—Get you something to drink?

—Coffee and orange juice please.

—You got it, hon.

As I look over the menu, I wonder what I'm going to say to Casey, and think again about the threat I'd received before leaving Ms. Newby's and the menacing phone call. How could sweet little Casey be involved with people like that? It was bad enough she was stripping—not in a moral sense, but in the having to deal with so many assholes sense. Like all professions, stripping has its troubled and lost souls, but many of the dancers I've met are strong, street smart, resourceful as hell, and shatter the Hollywood stereotype. I hope, like Regan, that Casey isn't getting caught up in the scene—the drugs, risky sex, further exploitation.

—Know what you want? the waitress asks as she places the coffee and juice down in front of me.

—Waiting for someone, I say. We'll order when she gets here.

On each end of the diner, not far from a security camera, an old fashioned round, wood-framed clock ticks off the seconds as I wait.

Through the rain-speckled windows, I can only see the lights of Bay Mini Storage—its lighted sign, and the red neon letters in the window that say, We Sell Boxes.

On Thomas the traffic is light and quiet—until bikers thunder by—the businesses beyond it closed, dark, unseen from here.

Three times while I'm waiting, headlights pan across the plate glass as cars pull into the lot, and I turn hoping it's her, that she somehow managed to get out of the house early, but as it turns out she is nearly a half-hour late.

When she walks in, I stand and move to hug her, but she extends her hand and I take it.

—Sorry, she says. Took longer to cash out tonight than usual.

She places her iPhone on the table and I notice it's just like mine—case and everything.

—No problem. I'm just so happy to see you.

—We have the same phone, she says. Don't you love it?

I nod.

—Can I get you some coffee? the waitress asks.

—Just water.

—You hungry? I say.

She shrugs.

—How about some heavenly hash? You gotta be hungry after working so late.

—Actually, the house mom had a ton of food in the dressing room tonight, and I already ate too much.

—Oh.

—But a little breakfast food sounds good.

The waitress returns with the water.

—What can I get y'all?

—Two strawberry pancakes and a slab of country ham, Casey says.

—And you?

—I'd like the hashbrowns topped with bacon and cheese, I say.

—Got it, she says. Get you more coffee?

—I'm okay, thanks.

I look over at Casey when the waitress leaves.

The dull ache the void of her absence had left in the center of me for the past three years has now become an intense, nearly unbearable pain. Shooting. Stabbbing. Searing. Seeing her, being this close to her again, has ripped open the wound that would never heal, and I sit across from her bleeding internally.

—It's so good to see you. I can't get over how grown you are, how good you look.

—I look like her, don't I?

I nod, unable to breathe for a moment.

—But, and I know she wouldn't mind me saying it, even prettier.

—Sometimes I'll pass by a mirror and for a split second think I'm seeing her.

She's right, I think. As difficult as this is, that she looks so much like Monica makes it more so—much more.

—I can't believe you're back in PC. How long have you lived here?

—About six months. I was gonna look you up, say hey, but just hadn't gotten around to it yet.

—How's Kevin? Do he and your dad live here, too?

—He's good. Huge now. I mean really, really big. But good. He's had some amazing teachers and therapists and he's on some pretty good medication at the moment. I know he'd love to see you.

—I'd love to see him. I really would. Think your dad would mind?

I can't even bring myself to say his name—Perry, a name I had grown to despise—using your dad to emphasize that the connection is to her and not me.

—Dad died about a year ago.

I'm shocked. How could I not know? Why hadn't she called? She's parentless and back in Panama City and hasn't reached out. She must be far more hurt with me than I even imagined. And who can blame her?

—What? How?

—Cancer.

—Oh, Case. I'm so sorry. I had no idea.

—Why would you?

—How are you?

—We're making it.

This is my fault, I think. My little Casey is stripping and having to take care of her burdensome brother by herself because I left her vulnerable, because I failed her, because I abandoned her.

—I want to help.

—We're fine. Really.

—But I want to.

—You don't have to. We're doing good.

Perry had prevented me from seeing Casey and Kevin, had relished the opportunity to excise me from their lives, to use them to get back at me for—what? Marrying Monica? Becoming a father to the kids he all but abandoned? He had kept them from me for the three longest years of my life. I am not sad he is dead—and yet, I am deeply distraught for Casey and Kevin, who have lost both their parents at such an early age.

—There's so much I want to say to you, to explain what happened and why things turned out the way they did.

—There's no need. It was a bad time for all of us. I understand. I really do.

The waitress arrives with our food, and Casey begins to eat. I just stir my food around, the guilt and pain suppressing my appetite.

—This is good.

—Good. The thing is, I say, I was so fucked up over what happened—and not just for the obvious reasons, but something far, far worse. And then your dad really didn't want me around or involved at all.

—Merrick, you really don't need to explain. I understand now. There's no playbook for shit like that. We all did the best we could.

She's never used my name before, and it's jolting. The little girl who had been my little girl for a while when her mom and I were married is no longer. The person sitting across from me is a woman, and I had missed the transformation.

Just seventeen when her mom died, Casey had still been very much a child. Now, barely twenty-one, she is every bit a woman—grownup in ways I would never be.

—I've got to go, she says. Kevin expects me to be there when he wakes up.

With the impediment of Perry out of the way and my head in a much better place, there's nothing to stop me from becoming a father to Casey and Kevin again. They are parentless. I am childless. We need each other.

—Are you in trouble? I ask.

—*What?* No. Why would you think that? Because I'm dancing at The Dollhouse?

—No. Thunder Beach.

She looks confused.

—Are you being harassed? I ask.

—What woman isn't?

—Casey.

—What? I can take care of myself.

—I had a guy tell me not to look for you tonight, I say. Actually threatened me. Another guy called.

—What? Are you serious? About me?

—Yeah.

—Who? How would they even know you were looking for me?

—I saw your picture on the Thunder Beach Magazine. It's how I knew you were in town. I asked around about you.

—Oh.

—Casey, what's going on?

—I have no idea. I swear. Lots of creeps in the world.

Whether she realizes it or not, she needs my help, and with Perry no longer around to interfere, that's exactly what she's going to get.

—You've got my number, I say. Please call me if you need anything. *Anything* at all. I can help. I really can. With bills, keeping Kevin—anything you need.

—I'll call you, she says. I will. We need to get you and Kevin together.

The door opens and Liz Jameson walks in.

—Just the man I've been needing to see, she says. Can I grab you for a minute before you leave?

—Sure, I say.

—Thanks, she says, and turns and takes a seat in a booth on the opposite end of the restaurant.

—Who's that? Casey asks.

—A truly amazing woman. She's sort of like a social worker. I did a story on her a few years ago. Done a few others *for* her since then.

—*For* her?

—Issues she deals with that the public needs to know about—mostly domestic violence.

She nods.

—You seeing anybody? she asks.

—Not so's you'd notice.

—Raven?

—Sometimes. Sometimes it's Regan.

She smiles.

—Any advice?

—I barely know her.

—But—

—I've really gotta go.

—Here, I say, taking out my wallet, withdrawing the two hundred dollars it contains, and giving it to her.

—Thanks, but I can't. We're good. Everything is—

—Please. For Kevin's medicine or sitter.

—Merrick, I made nearly twelve-hundred dollars tonight.

—Still. Please. For me.

—Okay.

She takes the money and I can tell she's doing it for me.

—Please call me. Please let me back in your life. I promise not to leave this time.

—You didn't leave last time, she says. We did. But I will.

She stands and I join her, this time grabbing and hugging her in spite of her outstretched hand. I hold her tight for a long moment, trying to make her feel my love. Like Regan after a shift, she smells strongly of cigarette smoke and sweet perfume.

For a while, she gives in to the hug, her body going limp, but eventually pulls back and begins to walk away.

—I'll call you, she says.

—Please do. I love you, I say, and for the second time tonight get no response to those words.

—**Y**ou workin' on a story? Liz asks when I walk up to her booth.

I shake my head.

—Good. I got one for you. Have a seat.

—There's a reason I'm not working on one right now, I say, sitting across from her.

—Yeah?

—Got downsized.

—You look the same to me.

I smile.

Liz has black curly hair and lots of it, and dark eyes and features that compliment it, and make her striking—even from across a room.

—Well, shit. Who am I gonna—

—Tell me what it is, and I'll find somebody for you.

—Thanks, Merrick. And, by the way, sorry you lost your job. If you need anything …

Though you wouldn't know it to look at her or by the work she does, Liz is one of the wealthiest people in town. Rejecting her family's money and power early in life, she dedicated herself to helping others after what she calls her Buddha experience. Eventually, she inherited all her family's wealth anyway, but continues on in her same job—only now with the resources to make a real difference.

—Thanks, but I'm fine, I lie.

Before losing my job, I was basically living paycheck to paycheck, and now I'm running through my final few hundred bucks. If I don't find a job soon, I'm not sure what I'll do. What I *can't* do, is borrow money from my folks. They're struggling as it is.

—What's the story? I ask.

—What is it always? she asks with a sigh.

—Man's inhumanity to man?

—Man's inhumanity to woman.

I nod.

—This spring break, we had more rapes, more assaults, more violence against women—hell, girls—than ever before. There's an escalation going on. I want to raise awareness and suggest some strategies.

—Okay.

—But I don't want the piece to have too narrow of a focus. You wouldn't believe the other shit I'm dealing with.

—Such as?

—I'm working with three different girls right now whose boyfriends—or monsters they thought were their boyfriends—have turned them into sex slaves. Good girls. All-American. Pretty—or used to be. One was supposed to meet me here tonight so I can get her back to Birmingham. She didn't show. I came back hoping she might still come.

—Where are they being held? I've got a cop friend who'd love to break down that door.

—They're not prisoners by force. It's far more subtle than that. The guy begins by isolating the girl from everyone. Then eventually gets her hooked on drugs or gets photos or video of her having sex—with him or others—and uses it to keep her from leaving. Says he'll show her parents and friends what a whore she is if she tries to leave. Then he moves her down here where she has no friends, no money, no … hope, and makes her earn him money on her back.

I shake my head, unable to process it.

—It's a fuckin' epidemic. You wouldn't believe the number of girls this is happening to—middle class American girls. Sure, some of the slaves are mail order brides who step off a plane and into a living nightmare, shuffled around the country from town to town, fucked by strangers, malnourished, drug-addicted, used up then thrown away, but a hell of a lot are cheerleaders and homecoming queens from decent families.

—I'll do the story, I say.

—What?

—Yeah. I had a chance to do a piece on something like this before and fucked it up.

—But—

—I've still got all my contacts. I can get it released on the wire services and I know several papers that'll carry it—even more than usual since it'll be free content.

—I'll pay you to do it.

—You most certainly will not. Will the girls talk to me?

She nods.

—When can I meet them?

—Give me a couple of days to set it up. I'll call you.

—I'll do background in the meantime. Have everything ready so we can shine a big fuckin' spotlight on these pricks, then ram it up their asses.

—I knew you were the right man for the job. Just don't make it too narrow.

—I'll start with the culture which allows, even encourages, man's inhumanity to woman.

As I prepare to pull out of Coram's onto Thomas Drive, headlights from a car in the Sonic parking lot across the street pop on.

Because of the threats I received earlier and the general strangeness of tonight, I turn right instead of left, taking a route that will enable me to circle around to see if I'm followed.

The car doesn't pull out when I do, and I decide I'm being paranoid, but just as I'm about to turn around, I see the headlights in my rearview mirror as the car enters Thomas and heads this direction.

I drive for a while, then take a left at Captain Anderson's and pull into the dark, empty parking lot. At the entrance of the restaurant, I back up to the fountain holding the enormous propeller of the Empire Mica, kill my lights and wait.

The Empire Mica was a British standard type Ocean tanker built in 1941 for the Ministry of War Transport at Haverton Hill, Teeside.

On June 29, 1942, while en route from New Orleans to the United Kingdom with a cargo of twelve thousand tons of clean oil, she was torpedoed by a German sub and sunk off the west coast of Florida, only fourteen of the thirty-three member crew surviving. Today the remains of the tanker lie some sixty-four miles from Panama City and twenty miles south of Cape San Blas in about 115 feet of water, her bow section still intact.

The propeller, mounted behind me now, was salvaged by Captain Laney Rinehart, who purchased the salvage rights to the vessel from the War Insurance Department for about a thousand dollars.

Laney's recovery of the propeller proved far more fraught with disappointment and drama than he ever could have imagined. He began in 1981, and with the help of Jack Pounders planned to blow the prop off the shaft. After two explosions, the huge propeller remained on the shaft. In June, Laney and his crew went back to the wreck, and after two more explosions, the prop was left lying in the sand. Later, he returned to the wreck with two twenty thousand pound lift bags. His plan was to lift the propeller, then tow it back to port. After rigging one of the bags, he discovered that the second lift bag had been sabotaged, and once again returned to port empty-handed.

For his next attempt, Laney hired a three hundred foot barge with a 190 ton crane, but when they dove the site, they discovered that someone else had already surfaced the propeller. He immediately reported the theft to the U.S. Marshall, and the propeller was located and impounded. Less than a year later, a federal judge ruled that the propeller belonged to Laney, and now it's hard to imagine the iconic Captain Anderson's Restaurant without it.

I smile.

People around here just think Laney Rinehart was stubborn. Wait 'til they see the lengths I'll go to in order to be Casey's dad again, to figure out what's going on, and keep her safe. Back when I was chasing down stories across the Panhandle, I kept a small .38 revolver under my seat, but with the loss of the job, I hadn't put it in my new car, and was regretting that now.

I see the beams of the headlights a few seconds before the car.

At first, it appears as if it will continue down the side road, passing the parking lot, but at the last minute it whips in and zips over to me, its high beams blinding me as it blocks me in.

Fumbling my phone out of my pocket, I try to decide if I should call Rashard or 911.

Unlocking the phone with a slide of my thumb, I hit the Keypad button, and tap in 9-1-1, thinking it quicker than calling Rashard directly.

Two enormous guys—one black, one white—both wearing jogging suits and jewelry, step on each side of my car carrying aluminum baseball bats.

Heart pounding, eyes bulging, throat constricting, I'm genuinely frightened.

The operator comes on as they begin to go to work on my new car with their sluggers.

—I'm in the parking lot of Captain Anderson's, I say, my voice high and tight. I'm being attacked. Send a patrol car. Now.

The car is more dent resistant than I would have thought, but they still do plenty of damage.

Surprisingly, they don't break the windows.

I can't hear the operator above the barrage of bat *thwacks*, so I hold up the phone so the guys can see it.

—Oh no, the guy on the left says. He's got a phone.

—The police are on the way, I yell.

—We tol' you to stay the fuck outta our business, the guy on the right says. The girl is spoken for. We see you again, won't be your car we bang on.

—We don't want the heat takin' you out'll bring, but we'll deal with it, we have to.

—These are not idle threats, my friend. Do yourself a favor and stay the fuck off the beach the rest of this week.

Then, in no particular hurry, they get into their car, back away, pull out of the parking lot, turn onto Thomas, and disappear into the night.

When, after another minute or so, the cops still haven't arrived, I disappear, too.

Driving away, I call Casey to make sure she's okay.

I can tell the call irritates her, but it's worth it. She is already safe inside her house and getting ready for bed.

I wake the next morning having not gotten enough sleep, and like every morning, check my phone for a missed call, a message, or a text from Regan.

Nothing.

Will I see her today? Will she call?

I can't remember ever being this way over a woman. Not ever.

When Monica and I were married, she was happy—happy to be with me, happy to be married. Even when it became obvious I wasn't, she never wavered in her devotion or desire—for me or the marriage.

Monica was so steadfast, so consistent, the intensity of her attraction never waning—no matter how much mine did. Regan's interest—or maybe it really is just her availability—is so inconsistent, so bipolar, it gives me insight into what Monica felt, what she went through, and only adds to my guilt.

It's been a while since I've even fallen for someone, but back when I had in what seems like a previous life now, I'd only ever do so much pursuing before I'd move on. I've never been the kind of person willing to convince someone they should want to be with me. I've always thought someone either wants to be with you or they don't. If someone is ambivalent, there's a reason.

With Regan things are different.

She's been as inconsistent as any woman I've ever been with, and though she's vacillated between intense interest and casual indifference, I can't let go.

I've started to several times—delete her number from my phone, avoid The Dollhouse, don't answer her calls. In fact, about two months ago I had ended it. And told her so—told her I could see she was conflicted and ambivalent and was going to leave her alone. And I did. Stopped calling and texting. Stopped going to the club … until I receive this text:

Thinking of u

Thanks. That's nice to hear. Of course I think of you, but less lately. I'm letting you go.

I'm sorry

For what?

4 pushing u away

Don't be. It's okay. I understand. I really do.

I miss u. Where will you be tonight?

In town, I text, though I had no plans of going before. Why?

I'll try to call.

She never called that night. But three days later she did and we got together—and have been on and off (at her, what? Whim? Schedule? Conflicted heart?) ever since.

She's not going to call today, I think. I should go back over to the beach and see what I can find out whatever Casey's mixed up in, not wait around just in case I might hear from Regan.

I decide to lie back down for a few minutes. I start to turn off my phone, but don't—and a few minutes later when Regan calls I'm glad I didn't.

We meet at the School of Fish restaurant in Windmark Beach right off 98 near Port St. Joe to avoid being seen by her husband or anyone who might recognize her.

Since Port St. Joe is only twenty minutes from Wewa, we're much more likely to see someone who recognizes me, but I don't care.

It's midmorning on a perfect May day, the endless expanse of sky bright and blue, dabbed with creamy cumulus clouds drifting by, the clean green of the Gulf, smooth and sun-sparkled, the breeze tinged with the scent of blooming flowers, fresh cut grass, a hint of brine beneath.

We have the small second-story porch to ourselves, and the place is mostly empty, still she keeps her shades on and glances around nervously.

The water and the sand and the sun and the resort-like atmosphere conspire to give our early lunch rendezvous the feel of a vacation— something we've fantasized about taking together.

She gets the Apalachicola oysters, gouda grits, and fried green tomatoes with remoulade. I get the blackened Gulf shrimp, cornbread, and roasted corn tarter sauce. It's a little early, but I order a Corona Extra with lime, she a glass of pinot noir.

When our waiter leaves, we sit in silence of a few moments, and I glance around, following the landscaping to the boardwalk to the beach and the white Windmark flags whipping in the wind.

—Somethin' wrong? she asks.

I shake my head.

—You sure?

—Yeah.

—You seem distant.

—Do I?

—Don't do that. Tell me what it is.

—Don't do what?

—You know.

I do, and I just need to say it. No games, no drama, just bring the truth.

—You mad at me for not telling you about Casey?

I shake my head.

—I understand, I say. You were in a difficult position.

—Then what?

—The whole time we've been doing this—

—What? Lunch?

—This. Us. I'm not sure what to call it.

—A relationship?

—The whole time I've been thinkin' the reason you seem like two different people is—

—I seem like two different people?

—Well, yeah. You don't think you do? I thought we talked about it.

—You mean when I'm at work and when I'm not?

—There's that, yeah, but—

—I explained that to you.

—No, you really didn't, but you didn't need to. I get it.

—Then what?

—The way you are with me.

—Which is?

—Sometimes it's so intense, so intimate, others you seem so … I don't know, casual, nonchalant, almost indifferent.

The waiter brings our drinks and bread—a small plate of powdered sugar-covered beignets. I wait for him to leave before continuing.

—This whole time I was thinking that it was because you're conflicted … you know … because of your … husband.

—Can we not do this now? It's such a beautiful day.

It is a gorgeous day. I look out beyond the planted palms of the resort to the sand hills and the pines shooting out of them, grateful the developers have left so much green, hoping as Windmark grows and expands they'll continue the trend.

—Then when? I hardly ever see you.

—Okay. You're right. Use his name. His name is Gabe. Say his name.

—I thought it was because you were conflicted about Gabe, but … now I'm thinking it might be something else.

—We talked about this. I *am* conflicted.

—And I appreciate that. I understand. You're a good person. But that's not enough to explain the two different yous I get.

—And you think you know what it is?

—Yeah. I think you don't love me. I can't believe I didn't see it sooner. When you really love someone, you … well, everything else just sort of dims, you know? It's like this new drug you can't get enough of. What's that line from No Good Man? I require love that's made of fire. It's just not like that for you.

—Can you really say what it's like for me?

—No, you're right. But you have so little time for me and—

—I've explained. I'm the only one bringing in any money right now. I have to work. I have to—

—I know. I do. And I've been nothing but patient and supportive.

—That's true. You have.

Gabe had lost his job, which is what forced Regan to return to dancing—something she hadn't done for several years.

—But I just got to thinking … I really believe we all make time for what's important to us.

—I make time for you.

—Sure. But compared to how much I—

—You have less to rearrange. More freedom. Less constraints.

—I realize that, and I've been happy to do—

Our food arrives, and we begin to eat.

—I'm happy to continue, I say, but … I don't know, I just thought, well maybe the reason you're not seeing me more than you are is that you really don't want to. You're fine if it works out and fine if it doesn't.

—If we're in different places, I continue, I'd just like to know. Like to adjust to … something more casual.

—It's not lack of desire or attraction, not for lack of wanting that I can't spend more time with you. It's not. I have very real limitations.

And I *am* conflicted. I'm just not … I feel so guilty sometimes, so … I've got to take this slow.

—That's cool.

Embarrassed, feeling exposed and vulnerable, I retreat into the very things I've been accusing her of—becoming aloof, distant, casual.

I can tell she senses the shift.

—I get it, I add. I do.

—You understand?

I nod.

—Yeah, totally, I say.

— *Totally?* She asks, a quizzical look beneath raised eyebrows.

—What?

—Nothin'. Let's just enjoy the rest of our time together.

—Sure.

We finish eating in relative silence, commenting only on how good the food is, how nice for us the development and restaurant are largely undiscovered so far.

As we're nearly finished, the crowd begins to pick up a bit. Across the way, on the other, larger porch, close to the bar, beneath the long hanging ceiling fans, business people noisily gather at the tables.

—Can we go? she asks.

I nod.

—I'm gonna walk down the back stairs. You can go back through the restaurant. I'll call you from the car.

She doesn't wait for my reply, just stands, and without a kiss or even a touch, she leaves our table, disappearing around the corner and down the stairs.

—I've always wanted to have a tryst at the Dixie Bell Motel, I say.

This is how I answer her call, as we're pulling out of Windmark.

—Okay, she says.

—Really?

—Really.

—Turn right on 98. It's down on the right. Mile and a half, two miles.

—You get the room then call me and give me the number.

—Thanks for doing this.

—My pleasure.

—It's most certainly going to be. I got mad skills that have just been languishing.

She laughs, a sweet, genuine, slightly wanton, seemingly involuntary laugh, and it floods me with an adrenaline-like spike of undiluted joy.

The Dixie Belle Motel, a fixture along Highway 98 in the heart of Florida's forgotten coast for as long as I can remember, is a '50s style roadside motor court where cars park right in front of the rooms. It's a tiny remnant of a bygone era, a last sliver of classic Americana. It appeals to me in so many ways, and that I get to experience it with Regan is like one of those rare moments in life when things actually work out the way we want them to.

Inside our small room, we are tentative and uncomfortable, glancing awkwardly at the two double beds.

—What happened to your car? she asks.

—I tell her.

—Oh my God. Are you okay?

I nod.

—What's Casey involved in?

—I'm gonna find out, but right now, let's forget about everything beyond that door right there.

—Sounds good.

—Come here, I say, taking her in my arms, beginning to slow dance with my ballerina girl, as I softly sing "Make You Feel My Love" in her ear.

— *When the rain is blowing in your face …*

She holds me tight as we move in a small circle, our bodies pressing into an ancient lover's pose, and I'm aroused to far more than just desire by the warmth and closeness of our embrace, and by her soft, sweet, impassioned breaths on my neck.

—Can you feel it? I ask. My love.

—I always feel it. Can you feel mine? I want you to feel mine.

— *When the evening shatters and the stars appear …*

—And not just when our bodies are touching, she adds, but—

My phone vibrates in my pocket, and she laughs.

—It's my phone, I say, but I'm also happy to see you. You mind if I get it? I told Casey to call me if—

—Of course.

—I just think she's in trouble and—

—Take it.

I do.

—Merrick?

—Yeah?

—It's John Milton.

—Hey Sheriff.

Regan's eyes grow wide and she takes a step back.

John Milton Parker has been the sheriff of Gulf County since before I was born. A lifelong friend of my father's, he's an honorable, gentle, tough Southern gentleman, a living legend of a dying breed.

—Where are you? he asks.

—On my way home, I lie. What's up?

—I need to talk to you. I'll meet you at your place.

—Something wrong? What is it?

—You call someone about a girl last night?

—Huh?

—Got a call from Frank McKeithen, sheriff over in Bay County. One of the models for the biker rally over on Panama City Beach …

—Yeah?

—Did you call about her?

—Yes, sir. Why?

—She's missing.

—**N**o one suspects you of having anything to do with it, John Milton says. Not Frank and not me. We're just following up leads. He knows I'm a friend of the family so he asked me to talk to you.

Speeding down Highway 71, I had tried Casey's number several times, but only got voicemail.

Before I rushed out, Regan promised to try her, too—and to see if she could get a line on where Casey and Kevin are living.

When I pulled up into my yard, the sheriff, who'd been leaning on his car in the shade of an ancient oak tree, stood up, and seeing the worry on my face, began to try to tell me I wasn't a suspect.

—You could've gone inside.

—It's nice out here—in the shade.

I live in a small clapboard house with a large screened-in porch beneath spreading oak trees on the bank of the Apalachicola River. The dwelling, more fish camp than residence, has been in my family for three generations, and though I've fixed it up a bit, adding some of the essentials, the best thing about it is what it doesn't have—a mortgage. This has always been nice; now it's an essential.

—What happened to your car? he asks.

I shrug.

—Don't know. I left it in the dark lot of an empty building last night at Thunder Beach. Came back to find it like this.

He eyes me suspiciously.

—How long's she been missing? I ask, trying to change the subject. I thought you guys didn't get involved until at least forty-eight hours.

—Don't really know any of the details of the case yet. Just told Frank I'd find out what you know and get with him.

—You wanna come in? I ask. Some tea or something?

He shakes his head.

From behind the house, I can hear a boat racing down the river, the mechanical whine of its motor, the wet *thwack* of the hull slapping the surface of the water.

—Why'd you call about her? he asks. Had you been drinking? The woman who works with the girls for the rally said it sounded like you were at a bar.

—I was at *Thunder Beach*. It's a little noisy out there.

—Oh.

—I saw the magazine and I thought I recognized her.

—And?

—I called to see if it was her.

—No, I mean who'd you—how do you know her?

—It's Monica's daughter, I say. Casey.

His eyes widen.

—Little Casey's on the cover of a magazine?

I nod.

—Such a shame about Monica and little Ty, he says.

A younger John Milton had been the one to find Monica and our son, Ty, the one to deliver the devastating news, the one to catch me as I collapsed.

I frown and nod, trying not to think about it.

We are quiet again, and from behind the house, I hear the loud *pop* of a pinecone falling from a tree and ricocheting off the tin shed in the back.

—What else can you tell me? I ask. Where'd she go missing from? Who reported it? Were there signs of a struggle?

—Don't know. Thunder Beach lady called Frank. He called me. I didn't know Casey lived around here.

—Me either.

—I'll know a lot more after I meet with Frank. See how I can help.

—When I asked around about her last night out at the beach, I was warned not to.

—That what really happened to your car?

I nod.

—Why didn't you just tell me?

—Sorry, Sheriff. I should have. I just … Hazards of my profession. Information management. Ask questions, don't answer them. Sorry.

—Any idea what she's mixed up in?

—None. I swear. What can I do to help?

—You know how these things go. You need to let Frank and his department handle it. But as soon as I meet with him, I'll call you and let you know what I find out. Okay?

He pulls out his card and hands it to me.

—If you think of anything else, give me a call.

Climbing into his car, he closes the door, cranks the engine, and rolls down the window.

—Tell your folks hello for me. And don't worry. I'll find Casey and get her back safely.

As soon as John Milton is gone, I try Casey again.

As I wait to be connected, I walk around the side of the house to the backyard, down to the river where the water slaps against the gnarled roots of cypress trees. In the midst of a particularly wet spring, the river is high, far more of the banks covered than usual.

The mid-afternoon sun refracting off the rippled surface of the river is blinding, and even with shades on, I can only look a little at a time.

When she doesn't answer, I leave another message, then call Regan.

—I need to know everything you can tell me about Casey.

—I honestly don't know much about her.

—Any idea where she lives?

—No.

—Who she live with?

—No idea. Sorry.

—She got a boyfriend?

—Not that I you know of.

—Anybody harassing her?

—Not that I know—wait. There was a guy. What was his name? Vic. Yeah. Vic … Victor Dyson.

—She meet him at The Dollhouse?

—No. He's the reason she left The Nugget.

—He was a customer at The Gold Nugget?

—Yeah. Starting harassing her. He's banned from The Dollhouse.

—What's he look like?

I had planned to catch a nap, go running, workout, and go by and see my folks, but instead climb in my battered but still beautiful new car and head down 22 into Panama City.

On my way out of town, I pass Granny's, a small biker friendly bar in a converted convenience store. The bikes filling the small lot and extending on the side of the road in both directions must number over a hundred, and I wonder how all the riders fit inside.

Highway 22 is a long, flat, slash pine-lined rural road, perfect for thinking or making calls.

Life in the Panhandle is spent racing down rural routes, and though most of the world's population now lives in large cities, there are still a lot of us who live in small or even tiny towns, connected by two-lane highways, well traveled by loaded log trucks taking pulpwood to paper mills.

Part of the reason Regan and I can meet without worrying too much about detection is we both live in small towns about the same distance away from Panama City—I in Wewa, she in Wausau—and come alone, mostly at night.

Like most of the roads in the area, 22 is filled with bikers going in both directions. I'm behind a lone rider with no helmet on a sleek black Yamaha Midnight Warrior, and watch with interest as he gives the biker wave to passing bikers.

I first noticed the special biker wave during Thunder Beach a few years ago and had included it in a story I wrote about the event. It comes from a time when there weren't nearly as many bikes on the road, when riding was far more countercultural, far less accepted than it is now. A sign of solidarity, the salute demonstrates support, but can also pass along information.

The most common wave, or at least the one I've seen the most, is the low wave—the left arm extended downward at a forty-five degree angle, two fingers out together if the rider is on a two cylinder bike, four if he's on a four cylinder, two fingers spread apart in the peace sign, or all fingers out for a low five.

For the piece I wrote, I was told some riders only wave to riders on the same brand of bike, while others don't wave at all, but I had never seen a biker not wave or receive a return wave in response.

Even as I think about bikers, my thoughts continually return to Regan, and it occurs to me that bikers are not unlike strippers in our society—both groups misunderstood, stereotyped, and clichéd by a self-righteous, Puritanical, clone-like culture, even as both groups have become increasingly mainstream.

Having lived and worked in the area for most of my life—as a reporter and more recently as an adjunct—I have a pretty good network of people I can call on to help track down Vic. As I race down the open, bike-filled road in a car I love, but will most likely have to soon part with, I begin calling in favors. I'd failed Casey before. I didn't plan on doing it again.

Rashard Little and I meet at The Gold Nugget.

Before becoming a Panama City Beach Police Officer, Rashard had been a correctional officer, before that a deputy with the Gulf County Sheriff's Department, and before that a star student and basketball player for Wewa High. Friends on and off the court, we had taken our small school to regionals three consecutive years.

Unlike The Dollhouse, which is a relatively new joint, The Nugget has been around so long my dad and uncles used to go to it when they were young men, and is the premiere gentleman's club in Panama City. I'd been to The Nugget a few times, but never during the day.

It's three on a Thursday afternoon, and the club is crowded, and I remember Regan telling me that the bikers in town for Thunder Beach hit the strip clubs in the afternoons. Like most places this week, in honor of the visiting bikers, the music being played is southern and classic rock, more outlaw, less rap and R&B.

Similar in setup to the Dollhouse, except with no playpen, the Nugget has two stages—a main and a gold—and a smaller round one against the far right wall called a satellite.

We sit at a table not far from the entrance.

Though there are two poles on each stage—the one in front of us and the one in front of the bar—there's only one dancer on each.

—Whatcha drinkin'? I ask Rashard, who is off duty and in street clothes.

—Bud Light.

The waitress comes over.

—Corona Extra and a Bud Light. Thanks.

I turn back to Rashard when she is gone.

—Thanks for meeting me, I say.

His gaze is fixed on the stage where a thin, tall, obviously athletic girl is doing some gravity-defying pole work.

—Thanks for asking me to meet you *here*, he says without looking away.

—I always say, why just get a drink when you can get a drink and see titties.

—Like the way you think.

The second song of the set starts and the dancers on the stages take off their tops.

—Got any singles? he asks.

I pull out about six and hand them to him, and he stands.

—Work that hard, you should get rewarded, he says, and heads toward the tip rail.

He steps through and around the bikers lining tables and standing near the stage, and waits his turn.

Racing heart, tension shoulders, anxiety mind—I want to rush things along, to force the action, but I've watched enough cops work and waited on enough stories to unfold to know you have to follow the flow. Rashard knows what he's doing. If you get in a hurry, you miss things, and ultimately do far more damage. I've just got to stop picturing Casey bound and gagged and vulernable.

As Rashard gets a kind of reverse motorboat, I scan the crowd. Looks like older regulars and visiting bikers, nearly as many women as men, and too few dancers for the number of patrons. I don't see anybody fitting Regan's description of Vic, but it's dim and her recollection was pretty vague.

By the time he returns, our drinks have arrived, and after he sits, he takes a long pull on his beer.

—Damn, damn, *damn*, he says. That's good.

I can't tell if he's talking about the dancer or the drink, but don't ask.

—See Teddy Bear over there? he asks.

I follow his nod over to the enormous bouncer near the DJ booth and the dressing room.

—Yeah?

—He's my cousin.

—Sweet.

—I called in and had the sergeant look up Dyson, he says. Got no record.

I frown and nod.

—But …

—But?

—Does have restraining orders against him from two different women.

I nod.

—No surprises there. Got an address for him?

He shakes his head.

—Been a while. He was living at a hotel at the time.

—Are the women wives, girlfriends, coworkers?

He nods toward the stage.

—Strippers, he says. Both blonde, built the same.

—Shit.

—Ain't it? Obviously, the trick's got issues, but I mean, goddam, it's easy to think these girls're into you. They're professionals at it. Many a loser leaves places like this thinking he all in love.

I look away, suddenly very interested in what the dancer is doing.

Teddy Bear spots Rashard and comes over.

—My nigga he says, after managing somehow to get his girth into the small chair.

They exchange knuckle bumps.

—'Sup big Bear.

—Just the price of a blowjob and my *got-damn* weight.

—You look good. Doin' your thing. Keepin' all these little honeys safe. Bear, this is Merrick. Merrick, Bear.

We nod at each other.

—We need your help. Lookin' for a guy.

He shakes his enormous head and flashes a blindingly white smile.

—Most people come in here lookin' for girls, he says. Gotta go to the Fiesta you wanna boy.

—Name's Dyson. He's—

—Vic the prick, Teddy Bear says.

—Yeah, I say. He been in lately?

—No and he won't be. Threw his bitch ass out a month or so ago and told him I'd break his fuckin' neck he ever come back. Why y'all need him?

—He's messin' with a friend of mine, I say. She used to work here.

—Who?

—Don't know what name she danced under. Real name's Casey.

—I remember Casey. She was cool as hell. No drama, no bullshit, no drugs. Felt like fuck for what he did to her.

—What'd he do? I ask.

—Typical bullshit. Trying to touch her, get special treatment, waitin' out by her car when she get off, followin' her. I woulda fucked him up for her, but she just left, never told anybody. Word got back through another dancer after she left. Part of the reason I fucked him up a little bit when I tossed him.

—Any idea where we might find him? Rashard asks. Any girls he may've given his number to?

—They wouldn't've kept it, so … I'd try Tan Fannies. It the only place he ain't been kicked out of.

Back in my car, I call John Milton.

Rashard is heading to work, and I'm heading to Tan Fannies.

—Hey, it's Merrick.

—You think of something?

—Just wanted to see if you found out who reported Casey missing yet.

I pull out of The Nugget, take a right on 98, heading east, then turn right onto Beck, toward St. Andrews.

—*Oh*, he says, you want information from *me*. I thought you were callin' to *give* me information—you know, since I'm charged with protecting and serving.

—I do have something for you.

—You do?

—Yeah, I say. What about the report? Who filed it?

—Don't know yet. Meet with Frank in a few minutes.

—What about where she lives?

—Who Casey? No one seems to know.

—How can no one—

—If she's living with someone else and everything's in the person's … So, whatta you got for me?

—Victor Dyson, I say.

—Yeah?

—I hear he was harassing her.

—Casey?

—Yeah.

—How'd you—

—Not important, but it's from a very reliable source.

—He a boyfriend?

—No.

—That's it? Not gonna elaborate?

—Don't know a lot.

I hope I won't regret it, but I just can't bring myself to tell him she's a stripper. If I have to eventually, I will, but for now, I think Rashard knowing is enough. Besides, it's not like John Milton will be very involved in the investigation anyway. So far, I'm the only Gulf County connection, and I don't think that's likely to change.

—You know more than you're telling me, he says. Been a reporter too damn long.

—Probably.

—Definitely.

—Or maybe you've been a cop too damn long. Got a suspicious mind. Think everybody lies.

—Everybody does. Okay, he adds with a sigh. I'll pass it along.

I'm about to turn onto Beck when I get a call.

It's Rashard.

—Got a lead on stalker boy, he says.

—Yeah?

—His mom's address.

—Great.

—Well, really she's his grandma, but she raised him. Don't know if he lives with her, but he might, and if he doesn't, she can probably tell us where he is.

—If she will.

—You kiddin' me? I can be very persuasive.

—I don't know, I say. You show up there in uniform and she's gonna shut down immediately. Let me go alone. If I don't get anything, you can always go back and try your persuasion.

—I don't know. What if he's there?

—All the better.

—You might not be as tough as you think you are.

—I'm Wewa tough.

—But—

—You know what Hank says. A country boy can survive. We can skin a buck and run a trotline. A country boy can survive.

—You might be a little country tough, but your ass can't skin no buck or run a trotline.

—Maybe, I can handle an old lady and a harasser of women. And can always call you if I can't.

He gives me the address.

—If he's there, he says, you call me. Fuck. I'm Wewa and ghetto tough.

I'm heading down 11ᵗʰ Street toward Vic's grandma's place at the Circle J when John Milton calls.

—There a reason Casey'd be using a different name? he asks.

—Don't know, I say, thinking she has a stripper name and is probably living under an alias.

—Bay County Sheriff's department can't find any evidence that she lives in town, and the name of the missing girl is different from—

—Probably trying to keep her identity a secret. Especially if this guy Vic's harassing her. What's the name?

—Amber. Amber Nicole Miles.

That didn't sound like a dancer name to me, but I'd find out from Regan what she uses.

—Probably just did it for security, I say. You find out who reported her missing.

—Yeah. An Ian King. Ring any bells?

—None.

—This thing's gettin' weirder by the minute.

As soon as we end the call, I punch in Regan's number, hoping to catch her before she gets home.

—Hey, she says.

—Hey.

—This is the most interaction we've ever had in a single day, she says.

—It's nice.

—It is.

—What name does Casey dance under?

—Tiffany. Why?

—Ever heard her use Amber or Nicole?

—No. Just Tiffany at the Dollhouse, but she could've used those others at The Nugget. What's going on?

—That's what I'm trying to figure out.

When I end the call, I begin to think about the approach I'll take with Mrs. Frankie Dean Chambliss, the woman who raised Vic "the Prick" Dyson.

Right after Ageless Book Shoppe and the Lunchbox and just before The News Herald, Circle J Trailer Court is across from Jinks Middle School on 11th Street.

Turning by the old rusting sign with the black J inside the blue circle and the red letters that read Trailer Court, I follow the narrow road between rows of extremely close mobile homes, over numerous speed bumps to the backside of the park and the small singlewide she calls home.

When I see the Jesus fish on her rusting Oldsmobile and the Ten Commandments sign in her tiny yard, I have my approach.

Standing on the cement steps, I pull open the flimsy aluminum screen and knock on the sun-faded door.

It takes a while for her to open, and when she finally does, I know why. Much older than I expect—even for Vic's grandmother—the stooped, shriveled woman doesn't walk so much as shuffle.

—Yes? she asks, squinting at me behind her grimy glasses.

—Hi, I'm Pastor Merrick McKnight, I say, using my real name in case she asks for identification. I'm the singles minister at Cross Bridge Baptist Church. I'm looking for Victor.

—He's not here right now. Whatcha need him for?

—He filled out a card for our singles program and I wanted to talk to him about getting involved. May I come in for a moment? It's heating up out here.

She nods and shuffles back.

Her chair is just a few feet from the door, and I wonder how long it would've taken her to answer if she'd have been in the back of the trailer.

When she finally reaches her chair, she doesn't sit so much as drop into it.

I come in and close the door.

The musty house is dim and in disarray, stacks of magazines and newspapers fill the floor while ceramic figurines and homemade knitted dolls fill all other surfaces.

Soiled seat covers creep off the old furniture—all of which is angled toward the small TV sitting atop the wooden cabinet of its predecessor.

With a shaky hand, she lifts the remote and pushes a few buttons until one finally turns off the TV.

—I've been telling Victor he needs to turn his life over to the Lord. I'm so glad he wants to be around other Christian singles. Maybe he could find a good Christian girl. That's what he needs. He's not a bad boy, but all young men need a good girl to keep 'em straight.

I had only guessed that Vic was single, but it was a pretty safe bet.

—I'd love to talk to him about it, I say. Where can I find him?

—I think he's out looking for a job. Usually doesn't get in 'til real late.

I nod.

—I worry about him so much. Pray for him all the time. If he would get in church and turn his life around … Don't get me wrong, he's not a bad boy, he's not. He's just … lost.

—We all were once, weren't we? I say. I once was lost, but now I'm found, was blind but now I see.

—Amen, she says, nodding her agreement and raising her hands in a worshipful pose.

—Don't you worry, I say, I won't stop until I find him.

—Thank you, preacher.

—No idea where he might be now? I ask. Where would he hang out when he's not looking for work? There a place he goes? A friend's house?

She shakes her head.

—I honestly have no idea, dear she says. He's so secretive about what he does with himself.

—Okay. Well, I'll keep trying back. What kind of car does he drive?

—A van, she says. He's a painter.

I nod.

—May I use your bathroom before I go?

—Well, of course, dear. Down the hallway on the left.

I walk down the narrow hallway that has no right, past the tiny bathroom and into what I had hoped was Vic's bedroom, but discover it's Mrs. Chambliss's.

Glancing around, I see that all the pictures are of her and a boy, then a teenager, then eventually a young man. I search until I find the most recent one—a dime store type portrait with a cheap background—take it out of the frame, fold it, and stick it into my pocket.

—You mind if I leave some literature in Vic's room? I ask, as I walk back into the small living room.

—He keeps it locked up so tight it'd take a SWAT team to get in, she says.

I nod.

—There's someone else I'm supposed to visit, I say. Thought he might be a friend of Vic's.

—Don't think he has any friends, she says. Stays to himself mostly. What's his name?

—Ian King. Have you heard him use that name?

Her lidded eyes widen a bit.

—Can't say for sure, but seems I have heard that name somewhere.

Tan Fannies is a topless club in the heart of St. Andrews. In recent years, the small downtown area had undergone a renewal, but as condos and specialty shops sprang up, some of old St. Andrews remained—pawn shops, oyster bars, and Tan Fannies among them. Next to the newly rebuilt, opulent Shrimp Boat, a block from the bright, sunny Uncle Earnie's, and just down from Oaks by the Bay, Tan Fannies looks more and more out of place every day—which only increases my fondness for it.

Driving back down 11th toward it, I had tried Casey again, but again got her voicemail and left another message.

When I pull open the door and step inside, I see right away that of the five people in the place, Vic's not one of them.

To my right, a female bartender stands behind the small bar, a grizzled gray patron in a dirty ball cap nurses a bottle of Bud at the far end.

To my left the pool tables are quiet, lonely.

Though there's a stripper pole and a small dancing area at floor level with a raised tip rail around it, the three strippers in various stages of undress are line dancing with an enormous boy with a huge belly in a two sizes too small T-shirt. The country song they're drunkenly dancing to pours from an internet jukebox on the wall behind them.

Everyone stops to look at me when I walk in.

—See your ID hon? the bartender says from behind the cash register at the end of the bar.

I pull it out and show it to her.

—What can I getcha? she asks as she hands it back to me.

I order a beer, step around the dancers and take a seat at the bar.

I nod at the gray man smoking and drinking his Bud, but he just stares at me.

The bartender is a middle-aged woman with below the shoulder wiry redish hair, overly tanned, sun-damaged skin, and enormous breasts bouncing beneath a scoop neck cotton shirt.

She places the beer before me and I overtip her.

—Thanks.

I nod.

She moves away to the register, and I turn to watch the dancing.

The roughest, most street-looking of the girls is leading the line dance, yelling out instructions between drags on her cigarette, pulls on her beer, and profanity-laced criticisms of her students' ineptitude.

The boyish-looking young man is panting hard, his barrel-like belly bouncing above his belted blue jeans.

—Wanna join us? the young blonde with a fishnet bodysuit asks.

—Haven't been drinking nearly long enough.

—Well, get busy, the tall middle-aged stripper with a mommy tummy, sagging breasts, big nipples, and a blue wig says.

I bring up my bottle and pretend to drink more than I do.

—Getcha another? the bartender asks.

I turn to face her.

—Not yet. Still working on this one.

This time she lingers.

—You seen Vic? I ask.

—Vic?

—Dyson. I was just talking to his grandmother, Mrs. Chambliss, and she's worried about him.

—You a cop?

Though the music is loud, it's not so loud that everyone in the building didn't hear the word cop and turn toward us.

I shake my head emphatically.

—No. Just a friend of the family.

—Vic ain't got no friends, Grizzled growls from the end of the bar.

—Of the family. His mom—well grandmother.

—Well which is it?

—Grandmother, but she raised him.

—We ain't seen Vic, he says.

—And we don't give out information about our customers, the bartender adds.

I nod.

—No problem. Just asking for Frankie.

—The fuck is Frankie? Grizzled asks.

—Frankie Dean Chambliss. Vic's grandmother.

I take a long pull on my beer, order another, and overtip again.

Eventually, the middle-aged mom with the blue wig goes over to the pole and begins her routine. Grateful for an excuse to move away from the tense situation I find myself in, I get some singles from the bartender and take my drink over to the tip rail.

With no DJ and no PA, the only source of music to strip to is the jukebox over between the restrooms and the lattice-enclosed VIP area. Often the dancers have to buy their own songs, which seems sort of sad to me.

I sit along the left side of the dance floor, so I can see the others and the door.

—I'm Mona. What's your name?

—Merrick.

—Cool name.

—Thanks.

I hand over a few ones.

She turns so her head is facing away from the others and speaks very quietly.

—Guy you're lookin' for's a creep.

I nod.

—You a cop?

—No. I'm really not.

—But you're not looking for him for his grandmother, right?

I shrug.

—He'll be in later tonight. Is most every night.

—Thanks, I say, then pull out a twenty, add it to the rest of my singles, and hand them to her.

—You find him, just fuck 'im up for me.

As I back away from Tan Fannies, I try Casey again.

While I'm in the process of leaving her another message, I receive a call from her phone.

—Casey? Are you okay?

—Yeah. Why? What's with all the calls?

Relief washes over me, and I can actually feel the physiological changes taking place. I pull into a parking space in front of the marina. Bobbing boats on black water, backlit by late afternoon sun.

—I'm so glad you're okay. I can't tell you how relieved I am.

I let out a long sigh, and can feel the tension leaving my body.

—Well, I am, she says, so you can stop calling every five minutes.

Her voice is tight, frustrated, angry.

—Where are you? What's going on? I ask.

—Whatta you mean?

—I want to help you. I told you I'm so sorry about what happened before, but—

—Merrick, I told you. I don't blame you for what happened.

—Well, I am to blame, but things are different now—and I want to help you.

—I know that.

—So let me.

—I will—when I need something. I don't right now.

—Case, the cops are looking for you.

—*What?* Why?

—They think you're missing.

—*Missing?* Why? From what? Why would they think that?

—Are you hiding from … someone? Something?

She doesn't say anything, her only response the quickening of her breath.

—What is it? I ask.

—Who reported me missing? she says.

—Why?

—There was a guy … you know … harassing me. I wonder if he reported me missing to get the cops to help him find me.

—Vic Dyson?

—Yeah. How the hell do you know that?

—I've been trying to find you. It's not him. He doesn't know where you live, does he?

—No one does. I'm a ghost.

—How can that—

—I use a PO box for everything. Got no utilities or anything in my name.

—Whose?

She is quiet a long moment.

—It's not that I mind you knowing. I just don't tell anyone. And with what's happening, you can see why it's a good thing no one knows.

I want to press her on it, but don't. I'm just easing back into her life. Don't want to push her away, scare her off. She obviously needs her privacy.

—Are you married? I ask.

—No.

—Boyfriend?

—Not at the moment. Had one, but he couldn't handle me dancing.

—He harassing you?

—No. And as far as Vic, part of my deal with The Dollhouse is he's banned. One of the bouncers walks me to my car. I'm very careful. I haven't seen him since I left The Nugget.

—Still want to talk to him. Is that okay?

—I guess.

—He could still be the one who reported you and just used another name.

—What name?

—Ian King. Mean anything?

—No.

—Have you ever used the name Amber?

—I've used a lot of different names. Some to dance under, others to give out if customers press me for my real name.

—Ever use Amber with Vic?

—Can't remember, but could have. Sorry.

—No problem. Okay. Are you safe now?

—Yeah.

—Can you stay put?

—For a while. I've got things I have to do tonight. Obligations. And I've got to work.

—Mind if I tag along?

—Actually, yeah. I do. I'm sorry, but I don't want you seeing me take my clothes off.

—I won't look.

She laughs.

—I've been looking out for myself and Kevin for a while now.

—Sorry about that. Wish I'd've known sooner.

—I'm good at it. I've got your number. I'll call you if I need anything. I promise. Okay? I've got to go.

—Be safe, I say, but she's already gone.

I follow the one-way street, pass the Shrimp Boat, Uncle Earnie's, The Watershed, the sun setting out over the bay, and make the block.

At the light, waiting to turn onto Beck, I call Rashard.

—She's not missing, I say.

—Say what?

—Casey. I just spoke to her. She's not missing.

—Where is she?

—Home.

—Where is that?

—I don't know.

—Huh?

—She's spooked. She was already hiding. Someone reporting her missing just confirmed she was right to be.

—But … Did you ask her?

—I did.

—She didn't want to say and I didn't press her.

—But that means we don't know for sure she's okay. Her abductor could've been making her say she was okay.

—Sorry. I didn't think I mean, she didn't sound under duress. I can call her back—or she said she was working tonight. I'll go by and make sure she's really okay.

—Well, I don't think we need to call off the search until we know for sure, he says, but it's not my call. Nobody knows I'm helping you.

—Yeah?

—We need to let Sheriff McKeithen know. His department is heading up the missing persons case.

—I can call Sheriff Parker from Gulf County, I say. I've been dealing with him. I can let him know so he can tell Frank.

—Sounds good. And you don't have to be in a big hurry to do it.

Doesn't hurt anything for them to be looking for her.

—I was thinking Vic could've reported her missing using a different name in order to find her, so I still want to find him.

—I'll be on the lookout for his van. We'll find him.

As I'm talking to Rashard, I get a text from Regan.

I'm in town. Where r u?

—Okay, I say to Rashard. I'll be in touch. I appreciate your help. And I'm really relieved. I think she's okay.

—Still need to find out what the fuck's goin' on.

—Agreed, I say and end the call.

On Beck, I type, and though I am so happy, so relieved that Casey's okay, I can feel myself lifting even more at the possibility of seeing her.

Want to meet?

Sure.

I have something to celebrate, I think. Casey is okay. I'm confused, but delighted and would love to spend a little time with Regan before continuing my search for Vic and trying to find out what's going on.

Where?

Where are you?

Can be in St. Andrews in 5.

I type, Watershed, Hunt's, Uncle Earnie's, Shrimp Boat, park, Tan Fannies, the coffee shop, marina?

Somewhere quiet. Private.

I think about it, then type in, Got an inspired idea. Park your car at the St. Andrews Marina and I'll pick you up.

OK.

I swing in Hunt's Oyster Bar for crab cakes and oysters, then by St.

Andrews Coffeehouse, in the old Gainer Brother's Grocery storefront, for java and sweets made by Emma Nell.

I know I should keep looking for Vic, and I will be again soon, but chances to see Regan are rare. Besides, I plan to ask her about Vic the prick and enlist her help.

A few minutes later, Regan, looking around nervously, gets in my car.

—What smells good? she asks.

—The new leather?

—That too. Such a shame what they did to your new car.

—Probably lose it soon anyway.

—I hope not.

I shrug.

—Don't seem too worried about it.

—Way down on the list of what matters.

—But you love this car.

—I was already reconciled to losing it, and with the way they've fucked it up . . .

—How's the job search going? she asks.

—It's not at the moment.

—You don't seem too worried about that either.

I realize I haven't shared with her my anxiety over losing my job and the financial crisis I'm in because of what she's going through with Gabe.

—I'm not, I lie. I'll find one soon.

Gabe has been without a job for a long time now—well over a year—with no real hope of finding another. If he's even really looking. I've been out of work less than two months, and could have a job tomorrow if I were willing to just take what I could find. Though in a similar situation, there are very few similarities in our respective predicaments, but I wonder if Regan sees that. Is this what's made her hesitant to go all-in with me? Do I seem like betting on another losing hand? I hadn't realized until this moment that Gabe and I have as much in common, at least on the surface surface, as we do.

—Whatcha got?

—Huh? Oh, a picnic.

—Where we goin'?

—Ever been on the deck behind FSU?

She shakes her head.

—Then you're in for a treat.

I pull around behind the FSU Panama City campus and park in the empty lot. After she's sure no one's around, we get out with the food and walk over to the deck beside the bay.

I had no idea this was back here, she says. It's beautiful.

They've torn part of it down. Used to be an amphitheater with built-in bench seating rising up which would've hidden us better.

Constructed of unvarnished wood planks and light poles, the enormous deck stands about three feet off the ground and is wrapped by a three-board railing, parts of it covered with a triangular, slanted wooden slats.

We walk up the ramp, onto the deck and look around.

The afternoon sun dances on the rippled waters of the bay, the blue expanse of sea and sky—dark below, light above—meet at the blue-black bruised horizon.

—It's so peaceful. Gorgeous.

She squints as she looks at the sun mirrored on the surface of the water, the breeze blowing in off the bay causing her hair to wave like the

Spanish Moss on the limbs of the oak trees around us.

We sit on steps leading down from the back side of the deck to the water's edge, not far from a pine tree with nearly its entire twisting root system exposed due to erosion, and I unpack the bags.

I dole out the food and we eat in silence for a few moments, watching the steady stream of traffic ascending and descending the huge hump of the Hathaway Bridge in both directions.

—This is so good, she says.

—All of it, I say. The food, the place, the company—not in that order.

We continue to eat, both of us working on the fresh, cold, salty oysters—cracker, oyster, hot sauce, gulp, repeat.

Behind us, the brick buildings of FSU are quiet beneath tall pines and expanding oaks. To our right in a small grassy area with trees at wide intervals, a gray-haired man walks a German Shepherd.

—So Casey's not missing? she asks eventually. She's okay?

I nod.

—You know anything about this Vic guy? I ask.

—The name sounds so familiar. Let me ask around tonight. I know I've heard it.

I shake my head.

—What?

—Sick fucks like this guy make me worry even more about you.

—I know how to handle myself—and there's always a bouncer around.

—Just having to deal with the hassle's bad enough, I say, but what about when you're not at the club, when you're by yourself?

—I'm never by myself. I try not to go anywhere without Pink.

—Pink?

She opens her purse and withdraws a small pink leather case for what looks like a pager.

—Pink, she says. My taser. It's small, but it delivers nine-hundred-and-seventy-five thousand volts.

—I'm glad you have it, but I'm still gonna worry. They're some fucked-up pricks in this world.

—I know. I'm careful. Thanks for worrying about me. But right now Casey's the one who needs worrying about.

—Worried about her, too. Anything you can tell me about her that might help me—or anything you think I should know?

—I'll think about it, but no, nothing comes to mind. She's a very good girl—smart, hardworking, straightedge, focused, you know? No drugs. No games. No drama. You should be proud of her.

—I am.

—So what's the story between you two?

—It's complicated. I was sort-of her stepdad for a while. I mean, I was—I was actually more like her real dad—but it wasn't legal. I didn't adopt her. I married her mom, Monica, when she and her brother, Kevin, were younger.

I shake my head.

—What? she asks.

—If I could change anything in my life …

—That would be it? What? Marrying her mother?

—The way it all turned out. Every bit of it. It was a short, unhappy marriage that ended so … Can we talk about something else?

—Sure. Okay. Like what?

—Anything but my biggest fuckups.

—Am I one of your biggest fuckups?

—You?

—Getting involved with me.

—Not at all.

—I know you stay frustrated with how … torn I am.

—Wanting more of you doesn't make me think this is fucked up.

—But what I do. Bet you never thought you'd get involved with a stripper. And then there's what you said last night.

—What's that?

—You know.

—Oh. That I love you.

—Yeah.

—Yeah?

—Do you really?

I nod.

—I do.

—Can you believe you're in love with a stripper? she asks.

I don't think of her as a stripper. It's not that it bothers me to. It doesn't. I think of her as a beautiful, graceful, kind, good person I find addictively attractive.

I'm not bothered by what she does, not jealous of other men admiring her, getting her attention, but I do want her treated with respect, want her given the dignity she is due. And too many customers don't.

What I feel for her, what she means to me, what we are together, is private. Secret. Sacred.

—I'm not in love with a stripper, I say. I'm in love with *you*.

—You're unlike anyone I've ever met, she says. I want you to know—

—Don't say anything about how you feel toward me.

—Why not?

—I don't want you feeling like you need to say it back or explain why you can't. I said it because I mean it, because I want you to know, and, for now, I'd really like to just leave it at that.

She leans in and hugs and kisses me, mashing the food containers between us.

—Thank you, she says. And thanks for being so patient, for not pressuring me, for being so understanding.

I think about all the ways I'm not patient and understanding, but realize I must mostly keep them to myself, managing to process my struggles instead of inflicting them on her.

—I don't want to, but I've really got to go, she says. Gabe'll be home soon.

I nod, and begin to gather the trash, feeling guilty at the mention of his name.

—This was so nice, she says. Sorry we got interrupted at the Dixie Belle.

—This was better, I say.

—Liar.

I smile.

—It *was* nice.

—But not as nice as getting naked.

—Nothing's that *nice.*

After dropping Regan off at the marina, I drive back down Beck and take a left on 98, heading out to the beach again.

Beyond the bridge and the buildings of the beach, the setting sun is sinking into the sea, the tangerine horizon is brilliant, too bright to behold for more than brief moments at a time.

Before me, bikes and riders are theatrical silhouettes driving into dusk, the roar of their modified mufflers ripping through the air, seeming to tear a hole in the fabric of the atmosphere.

Pulling out my phone, I tap in John Milton Parker's number, carefully, keeping an eye out for the ocean of motorcycles my banged up deep water blue challenger is swimming in.

—Hey, Merrick.

—Sheriff.

—What can I do for you?

Anytime someone asks me this—particularly early in a conversation—I feel like I'm interrupting and need to rush.

—Are you still with Frank?

—Back in my office, trying to catch up. I'm out of it—unless something changes. I helped with some background on Casey, but wasn't much I could do. What's up?

—I just heard from Casey.

—*What?*

—Yeah. She says she's not missing. Never was.

—Are you sure?

—About what?

—That it was her. Did you see her?

—No. Just spoke on the phone.

—Can you go by and see her for yourself? Take a deputy with you so we can—

I explain to him why I can't.

He's quiet for a moment.

—I understand why she would feel that way—'specially with what's goin' on, but we've got to know that she's okay. What's her number?

I find it in my phone and give it to him.

—Let me call her first and explain the situation and why I had to give it to you, I say.

—Just go ahead and do it. I'm gonna call Frank now. He'll move on this fast.

—Okay. Do you think someone trying to find her could have reported her missing? I ask.

—I can't figure out what the hell's goin' on. Makes no sense to me whatsoever. It's not my case. Smarter people than me are working it. I just want little Casey to be all right.

—I really think she is, I say. And I want her to keep on being that way.

When he is gone, I call Casey. Getting her voicemail, I leave her a message explaining the circumstances under which I felt compelled for her safety to violate her trust and give her number to the police, asking her to please understand and call me as soon as she can.

While in the middle of leaving the message, Rashard calls. When I finish, I call him back.

—You won't believe this, he says.

—What's that?

—I was called to quell a little disturbance in the Days Inn parking lot on Front Beach.

—You're right, I say. I can't believe it.

—Funny. Anyway … apparently some non-biker tourists took offense at the thunder coming from bike mufflers and decided to let some of the bikers know it.

—That the part I won't believe? 'Cause I've got no problem swallowing that either.

—So I'm in the parking lot—

—Quelling, I add.

—And I glance over at the Karaoke bar across the street.

—Sweet Dreams? I got drunk enough to sing there like a decade ago.

—Glad I wasn't there, he says. Can't get drunk enough to hear that. Anyway, so guess what's in the parking lot?

—Probably not bikers, I say. Half naked teens with rock star dreams?

—An old white van. Guess what's on the side?

—What?

—Dyson Residential and Commercial Painting.

—Doesn't mention anything about his sexual harassment services?

Beneath the ubiquitous yellow background, black letters LIQUORS sign, looms another of the same size with red letters and a white background that reads SWEET DREAMS KARAOKE BAR. Like everything on the beach, the signs are competing with thousands of others, jammed together not dissimilar to the buildings behind them so it all appears to be one continuous business—and in a way it is. The business is tourism, the entire beach one giant, gaudy strip mall with shiny trinkets and firewater.

On the way out I called Casey and Regan again, twice, but was unable to reach either of them and received no return calls.

I have to park further down 98 in front of The Plaza Motel beneath a sign threatening to tow non-customers, and by the time I reach Sweet Dreams, Rashard is coming out from beneath the blue awning of the package store side.

We step over near the ice machine to keep from standing in the way of people and their liquor.

—Don't think he's here, but don't know what he looks like so …

Unlike earlier, Rashard is now in uniform, and the transformation is palpable. The crisp black uniform compliments his dark skin, and his leather belt holds so many gadgets in addition to his gun, it looks like it could belong to Batman.

I pull out the folded picture of Vic and hand it to him.

That him?

I nod.

—Recent?

—Not sure, but I think so.

He shakes his head. Pretty sure this guy's not here.

—You check in the van?

He nods.

—Couldn't see all the way in the back, but banged on the doors. Pretty sure he's not inside, but not positive.

I look at the old van again. To my surprise the phone number on the side is not a cell. I can tell by the prefix that it is a local land line.

—You try the number? I ask, pulling out my phone and programming it in.

—Answering machine. Didn't leave a message.

Immediately inside the door of Sweet Dreams is the DJ booth. It sits on the left wall across from the ATM, is raised, and has an opening so the DJ can check IDs and take Karaoke requests.

I whip out my license, but with Rashard in uniform, he nods us on through.

—Seen this guy? Rashard asks, holding up the picture of Vic.

—He's in here earlier.

The DJ is a forty-something, skinny white dude with an acne-scarred face and a blond-gray ponytail.

—He left?

—Yeah.

—Get in his van? I ask.

The DJ looks through the glass door at Vic's van and shrugs.

—Don't know. It's still here. Probably walked down to the Red Door. Think he's got a thing for bikes.

—You know him?

He shakes his head.

—Just saw him checkin' 'em out. Looked like it gave him wood.

—Keep an eye on the van, Rashard says. Holla at me if he comes back.

—Sure, man. Okay.

We step through high tables with black chairs, all of which are empty except for two, and over to the bar running down the right side of the room. Above us, beer banners hang from the black ceiling next to PA speakers and Karaoke monitors. Around us, the black and blue walls have large mirrors of varying shapes surrounded by white rope lights.

On the small stage along the back wall, a squat, rotund white guy in shin-length shorts, bright new tennis shoes, and an enormous T-shirt with some sort of sports equipment logo on it sings a country song I've never heard before. He has a black mullet, a Vandyke, and a large gold earring, and it's obvious he thinks he sounds better than he does. From a table near the stage, two girls and a guy cheer for him and snap pics.

The bar is mostly empty, too, save three thirty-something bleach blonde ladies sitting at the far end, laughing loudly with each other and whoever's on their cell phones.

—What's occurring? the large lady bartender asks Rashard in a surprisingly thick British accent.

Dressed in black, she has very pale skin and dyed black hair.

—How you doing? he asks.

She frowns and shrugs.

—Ain't gonna lie to you, copper. Could use some more business, I could.

—This guy been in tonight? he asks, placing the picture on the bar.

She studies it, then shakes her head.

—Can't say as he has, she says, no.

—So your DJ's lying? I say.

—Huh?

—Look again, Rashard says. His van's parked out front.

She lifts the picture and angles it toward the light from the cooler on the wall behind her.

—Didn't get a proper look at it before, did I?

As the country song ends, rotund stumbles down from the stage and is replaced by one of the girls from his table. The DJ announces her as Gwen just before Hit Me With Your Best Shot begins to play.

The bartender studies it for a moment longer, then shakes her head.

—Can't say for sure, she says. Could be the sad bloke what sang the crackin' song from Rocky Horror Picture Show. But just as likely not.

—If it's him, I say, know his name?

She shakes her head.

—He come in a lot?

—I ain't been here long, have I?

—In the country? Rashard asks.

—At *this* pub, she says.

She hands the picture back to Rashard who hands it to me. Pulling out a card, he tells her to call if Vic comes back in.

She nods.

—All right then. You lot can count on me. She turns and places the card beside the phone. Put it right by the phone, she says. He comes in, I see him, I call you, and Bob's your uncle, you'll nick your man.

Back outside, we stand beneath the faded blue Sweet Dreams sign on the face of the building and discuss our options.

—Can't you jimmy your way in? I say.

He laughs and shakes his head.

—Sure. I can just shoot him when I see him, too. We don't even know if he's done anything.

—Oh, he's done plenty. Not easy gettin' banned from strip clubs.

Rashard gets a call on his radio and steps a few feet away to take it.

I step out, past the van to stand near Front Beach. Between the myriad motorcycles roaring by, carloads of teenagers creep along, windows down, heads hanging out, yelling, screaming, whistling.

The slow-moving traffic stretches as far as I can see in both directions, disappearing into the night. Behind the condos and houses and hotels, the rolling tide of the unseen Gulf, shrouded in darkness, can't be heard above the din of engines and horns and radios.

I turn back to look at Rashard. He's involved in an intense conversation on his cell phone. Behind him, rows and rows of liquor bottles can be seen above the white lattice inside the plate glass, neon logo signs making the well-lit package store look like the possibility of a party in paradise.

When he gets off the phone, I walk back over to him.

—Gotta go, he says. Being dispatched to a bar fight further down the beach. Tried to get out of it. Hell, even tried to take the rest of the night off, but with Thunder Beach, just can't do it.

   —No problem. I appreciate your help.

   —Whatcha you gonna do?

   —Think I'll hang around here for a while, see if he comes back.

   —Call me if does, okay? Don't talk to him without me.

I nod.

   —Sure, I say, as if I really mean it.

As I move my car from the Plaza Motel to the Paradise Palms and park directly across the street from Vic's van, I try Casey again. Since having to give her number to John Milton, I had been trying her periodically. When I get her voicemail, I leave another message.

My phone beeps to let me know the battery is nearly empty, and I search around for my charger. Once the cigarette lighter is providing the needed juice, I call Regan.

It's eight-fifteen—usually the time she's driving to work and can take my call, but she doesn't answer.

It frustrates me, and I realize it's not my inability to reach her this evening, but what this has meant in the past—her pattern of intimate connection followed by withdrawal.

Why can't I just let go?

Is it that her pattern of cutting me off after having given me some of the connection I so long for has me addicted? Is the unhealthy dynamic actually feeding the flame of desire? Or does the deepest part of me—my what? Soul? Essence?—know something beyond thought, beyond reason? Of course, I want to think it's the latter, but can't help but worry it's the former.

I sit for a while longer, then remember the DJ saying Vic may have walked down to The Red Door Saloon. Leaving my car, I cross over Front Beach, winding my way between the slow moving bikes, and head west.

The night is alive and loud—idling bikes, yells, whistles, horns. There's movement everywhere—people walking up and down the sandy shoulders of the road, popping up through sunroofs, hanging out car windows, leaning over hotel balconies.

I walk down 98, passing the Plaza, crossing over Laurel Street, in front of Noah's Ark—the Christian concert and rec center with a facade of the famous biblical boat, and to The Red Door.

The place is packed, the lot lined with bikes, the porch and bar standing room only. Smoke rises, drifts, hovers. Music blasts. Cups and bottles are raised. People talk and yell and touch—hand clasps, knuckle bumps, bro hugs, dry humps.

It takes a while to search the crowd, but eventually I leave fairly sure Vic's not among the throng. I become certain when I get back to Sweet Dreams to find his van gone.

Angry at myself for leaving, I pull out of the Paradise Palms heading west, scanning for Vic's van as I creep along in the playtime processional.

In addition to straining to see if the van is in the traffic, I glance through the parking lots of the bars, bike shops, tattoo parlors, Moped rental places, T-shirt tourist traps, pizza and seafood places.

Just past Black Cat, I turn and head back east, figuring he's most likely returning to town.

The crawling traffic is filled with more motorcycles than cars, and it takes a long time just to make it a mile or so.

When I reach the site where Miracle Strip used to be, I take a left, deciding to cut over to Back Beach in order to get back into town faster.

And that's when I see it.

As I turn by Alvin's Island, I spot Vic's van in the very back of the parking lot between Alvin's Arcade and the mini golf course near Shipwreck Island Water Park.

I whip into the parking lot, and pull into a spot not far from a giant Jaws-like cement shark coming up out of one of the holes at Shipwreck Golf.

Getting out of my car, I look across the street and, not for the first time, mourn the passing of Miracle Strip. I'm surprised to see how many buildings remain behind the overgrown lot and fence.

Suddenly, I'm a teenager again, back at the amusement park on a hot summer night, the sweet smell of cotton candy and caramel apples drifting through the thick, humid air. Screams of excitement come from every direction—the Starliner as it rockets down the first hill, the swings spinning around so fast they change from vertical to horizontal, the Music Express slinging riders to the inside of their seats—all to the soundtrack of rock and roll, screeching metal, hydraulics, carnival games, organ music, whistles, yells, and honking horns coming from 98.

Fronted by planted palms, Alvin's Island Tropical Department Store is housed in what looks to be a giant reddish clay rock formation.

Known as Alvin's Magic Mountain Mall, the retail outlet, which has been on the beach for nearly sixty years, is a cave-like labyrinth of beach towels, bathing suits, toys, T-shirts, caps, hats, purses, stuffed animals, gator heads, and every conceivable glass and ceramic and plastic souvenir—all branded with Panama City Beach.

I wander around the rows and rows of trinkets and treasures, the shelves and shelves and shelves of T-shirts and towels looking for Vic. Upstairs and down, in and among shark tanks and live alligator photo opps, between and around sunburned tourists, white strap marks on their shoulders, pale sunglasses stencils on their red faces.

I search for nearly an hour—popping out to the parking lot often to ensure his van's still there—but no joy. No Vic.

When my phone vibrates in my pocket, I step outside to take the call, not wanting to attract any attention to myself in case I missed him and Vic really is in the store.

The dark night is lit by neon and halogen, and though it's not raining like last night, the approach of a storm can still be felt in the atmosphere.

—Hello.

—Merrick?

—Yeah?

—It's Dan.

Dan Alton is a reporter for a daily over in Destin. We'd worked a few stories together and had become friends.

—Hey, man. How are you?

—I'm okay, he says. You?

—Not bad.

—Heard you got the boot.

—You heard right, I say.

I think about how many journalists are losing their jobs. Every week brings news of another daily shutting its doors, of the end of an era, as advertisers pull their dollars from printed news, where journalism in America is dying a not-so-slow death. It's a true tragedy, one that threatens our democracy as much as anything else. And it's not just that professional journalism is in ICU, but more so that people are getting their news from crackpot partisan blowhards meant to bolster what they already believe and comedians who go for a laugh above all else, including the truth, but that We The People have stopped reading.

It makes me sad and angry. It also causes me great concern for our future. People don't seem to realize what's at stake. Studies have shown that in cities where newspapers close, less people vote in elections, incumbents stay in office longer, and members of congress don't work as hard for their constituents, don't funnel as much money back home, and more often vote along party lines.

—I did, too, he says.

—You got fired? Shit, man. Sorry to hear that. Why?

—They found a kid who'd do it for half the money.

—If they only knew the real price they're paying, I say. Sorry.

—No, it's all good. It's why I'm callin' you.

—Yeah?

—Yeah. A group of us *former* print journalists are starting an online publication.

As more and more dead tree editions of papers are dying (filing bankruptcy or disappearing)—some, like the Rocky Mountain News in Denver, after 150 years—online editions are springing up to fill the void. Something similar happened in the publishing industry—independent presses springing up all over the country to publish books the conglomerate-owned New York houses no longer had room for among all their celebrity titles.

—Really? I say.

—Yeah. It'll cover most of the Panhandle—especially the Emerald and Forgotten Coasts. We'll pick up the slack from the dailies and weeklies closing or laying off their most experienced reporters.

—Very cool. That's exciting, man. I'm happy for you.

Thomas Jefferson once said something like if it was left to him to decide whether we had a government without newspapers or newspapers without a government, he wouldn't hesitate to choose the latter. Smart man. Of course, he was probably running a newspaper at the time, and changed his tune later when he was in government, but most people don't get it. There's a huge disconnect between the role of newspapers in civic life and what citizens perceive them to be. A recent poll found that only 43 percent of Americans said losing their local newspapers would hurt civic life; 33 percent said they would miss reading their local paper. If they knew the differences in the way judges judge, the way businesses do business, those numbers would be 100 percent.

—We want you to join us, he says.

—What?

—You can be a full partner in the venture, own part of the company, help us launch it, or you can be one of our top guns for hire. Either way, we want to put your experience to work for us, for this area.

I look over at the large ENTRANCE sign and the few remaining buildings of Miracle Strip—overgrown, boarded up, remnants of an earlier era—and think it's not unlike American print journalism.

When I don't say anything, he clears his throat.

—Whatta you think? he asks.

—Sounds very interesting, I say.

But it's hard for me to think about much of anything right now. Maybe when I know for sure Casey's safe I can really consider it. I've got to do something soon. I'm running out of the little money I had fast.

—It's the real deal, he says. The future—and it's here now. Look, we have investors. We can pay you. Probably won't be as much as you were making before—

—Be a hell of lot more than I'm making now, I say. No matter how much it is.

—And if you join us now, you stand to make a windfall later on.

—It sounds great. Really does.

—I want to set up a meeting. Let you see who all's involved, our plans, all the details. Just don't rule it out until then. Okay?

—I won't.

—Okay. Great. That's great. I'll set something up and be in touch.

—Thanks, Dan. And thanks for thinking of me.

I climb in my car, recline the seat, and settle in to watch Vic's Van until he returns.

I think about what Dan said and feel a certain excitement about the possibility of chasing down stories again, of being part of something new and cutting edge.

As if an obsessive-compulsive's ritual, I call Casey and Regan again. Neither answer, and I don't leave messages. They're probably both working. When they check their phones on a break or, if they're really busy, when their shifts end, they'll see I called. Doesn't mean I'll hear back from either of them. Probably won't.

Eventually, I drift off, and soon I am dreaming.

Images of an earlier time.

Endless summer night. Shimmering heat. Sweat-tinged skin.

Miracle Strip. Flashing lights. Spinning rides. Swelling music. Pulsating. Pounding.

Monica. Happy. Nauseous. Pregnant.

Teenage Casey. Faded jeans. Boyfriend's Bay High Wrestling Team T-shirt.

Eight year-old Kevin. Wild-eyed. Over-stimulated. Manic.

—Let's do the rollercoaster again, Casey says.

—You know, you know, you know what I want to do? Kevin stammers. Merrick McKnight. Hey Merrick. Do you know what I want to do?

—What's that buddy?

—I want to ride the cars. Can we do that? Can we? Let's ride the cars, okay?

—Sure, Casey says. That's fine.

Because of Kevin's autism, Casey had spent her life acquiescing, deferring, accommodating, and never complaining, so I had always attempted to take care of her, make sure she got to have some semblance of a childhood, too. With Monica pregnant, it meant I was the lone chaperone for rides.

—You sit here with Mom, I say to Kevin, while Casey and I ride the rollercoaster, then I'll take you over to the cars.

—But I would like to go *now*.

—It's fine, Casey says. Really.

—Thank you, I say, but we're going to ride the rollercoaster first, then the cars. Kevin, sit here with Mom and we'll be right back.

—But, but, but, I don't want to sit here. I want to ride the cars. I want to ride the cars right now.

—It's Casey's turn, then yours. We just rode the biplanes for you. I'm going to ride the rollercoaster with her, then I'll ride the cars with you. That's the way we're going to do it. If you get upset you'll have to go, so sit here with Mom. Okay?

I can see by his agitation that this can go either way. Will he meltdown or sit down? There's no way to predict.

—I really like the cars, he says. Like them a lot. A lot. Want to ride them now. Right now.

He continues saying how much he likes the cars and wants to ride them even as he sits down on the gliding swing besides Monica.

—Thank you, Kevin, I say. We'll be right back.

Casey smiles up at me, and as we turn to head over to the Starliner,

Monica grabs my hand and pulls me back.

—I'd love and adore you if it was just the two of us, she says, but the way you are with my—*our*—children makes me worship you.

I wake with a start.

It's late, the night dark, empty, the beach abandoned.

I sit up in my seat, angry at myself for falling asleep, and realize my phone is vibrating in my pocket.

Pulling it out, I turn my wipers on to remove the dew from my windshield and confirm Vic's van is still here. It is. In fact, his and mine are the only two vehicles in the lot.

Glancing at the display on my phone, I see that it's Casey.

Hey, I say, then clear my throat in an attempt to get the sleepiness out of it.

—Merrick?

—Yeah?

—What's wrong?

—Whatta you mean?

—What's with all the calls and messages?

—I just wanted to make sure you're really okay.

—I am. I told you. We've been through this, she says, her voice ragged, impatient. I told you, I'll call you if I ever need anything. Please stop calling. You're freaking me out.

—Sorry. I was just worried.

—Well, don't be. I'm a big girl—can take care of myself. I'll let you know if I need anything. Okay?

I nod as if she can see it.

—I've been patient, she adds, but I really mean it.

—Okay.

—Good.

—But I'd like to see you in person.

—What? Why?

—Just to make sure you're not being made to tell me you're okay.

—I'm at work. You can stop by if it'll … her voice changes, moving away from the phone. Huh? Oh. I'm up next. Got to go. Remember what I said. I'll call if I need you.

I start to say something, but she is gone.

—**S**o swing by work and see her, Rashard says. Know for sure.

—Yeah?

Though his call is just a few minutes after the one with Casey ended, I had already dozed off again.

Eyes stinging, head hurting, throat scratchy, I pop open the glove box, withdraw the small, plastic tupelo honey bear, tilt my head back, and squirt a large dollop of the thick, golden elixir on my tongue. Old timers around Wewa had always sworn by the healing powers of honey—particularly tupelo. As a kid, I thought it a wives' tale, but the older I get, the more convinced I am it's true. The sweet medicine is soothing to my throat, and makes me realize how hungry I am.

—And whatever Vic the prick's up to out here, got nothin' to do with her if she's in town at work, he continues.

—Guess not—or not directly, or not at the moment. Still want to know what it is.

I look over at his van, then scan the area again. No sign of him—or anyone else.

—The fuck you still doin' out here? Go. Go check on Casey, then go home. Go to bed.

—What about Vic?

—Prick's on my radar now. Safe money says he'll be in jail before Fourth of July.

I drop by The Dollhouse just long enough to make sure Casey is okay, and though Regan's car is in the lot, I don't see her, and I'm glad.

Casey is even more annoyed with me than before.

—See, she says, waving her hand across her skimpily clad body, I'm not missing.

We stand not far from the bar, near the reception counter.

—Sorry, I say. I know you don't want me seeing you like this, but I just had to be sure.

My relief that she is okay supersedes my awkwardness at seeing her in what amounts to little more than bra and panties, but I keep my eyes locked on hers, not looking anywhere else.

—Doesn't matter, she says. And what if it did?

Those words, that question, sounds so world-weary, so futile, so fatalistic, they break my heart, and cause me more guilt than she can ever know.

—I'm just trying to look out for you, Case.

—Like you used to, she says.

And should have never stopped, I think.

—I tried, I say.

—No, you *did*. But that's been a while. I'm not a kid anymore.

—Obviously, I say, nodding toward her body, though never taking my eyes off hers, but you *are* in danger.

—You … Are you …

—What?

—You sure you're not just trying to make up for …

She's right, and I know it, but this isn't just me attempting to exorcise regret.

—Guys warning me not to look for you, ones treated my new car like a piñata, and whoever they work for, shouldn't be taken lightly.

—Then I won't. I've got to get back to work. Regan's in the VIP if you wanna wait.

I leave relieved and frustrated, guilt and remorse feeding on the fringes of my thoughts. In the car I crank up the dance music from La Vela on PFM, attempting to keep from falling asleep on my long drive home.

I fall into bed as the sun is coming up, and sleep too much of the next day away. Maybe if I hadn't, I could've prevented what happened, but Casey wasn't the only one I failed to convince just how dangerous things really were.

I wake feeling restless and frustrated. It's as if I'm sleep deprived and hung-over, though I'm neither.

I don't feel like doing anything, but I force myself to get up, read, think, jog, workout, and shower.

In between each activity, I check my phone, and a few times I call or text Regan.

By the time I've finished everything, it's mid-afternoon, and still no response.

Eventually, I climb into my car and head back out to Thunder Beach to hang around the events, to be close by in case Casey needs me. Of course, it means that if Regan calls and says she's in town, I'll be close enough to meet her with just a few minutes' notice.

Bikes everywhere.

The traffic is much heavier now, every other vehicle a bike.

Not having eaten since the oysters and crab cakes with Regan the evening before, I'm famished, but I manage to hold out until I can stop by Cahall's on 23rd Street for one of their legendary chicken salad sandwiches, then by Gaston's downtown for a piece of fresh strawberry cake.

The slice of cake is so good, I have a second, while talking to Gaston about the upcoming UFC fight he's showing on his big screen the following weekend. Promising to return for the match, I get a third piece and a cup of coffee to go—he even lets me take a mug when I promise to bring it back soon.

When I finally make it to the beach, I stick to the official Thunder Beach venues—Boardwalk, La Vela, Sharky's, Sandpiper Beacon, Pier Park, Frank Brown Park, Edgewater, and Rock'it Lanes.

Moving slowly from place to place, I look through the seemingly endless line of vendor booths, live music playing in the background.

There are exhibits, demonstrations, stunts, drill teams, bikini bike washes, Show Us Your Tats and Rate The Rack contests, poker runs in progress, lingerie shows, and every kind motorcycle known to mankind.

I arrive at The Boardwalk in time to see the Miss Thunder Beach pageant finale.

Miss Thunder Beach began as a bikini contest—always one of the most popular events of the rally—but has grown into a full scale-pageant series with a spokesmodel program.

Truly beautiful women with amazing bodies are walking across the stage in skimpy, sexy bikinis, and I can't imagine the judges saying that one looks better than the others. But that's exactly what they do.

Thankfully, Casey isn't among them. Making herself scarce is the safest thing she can do right now.

Following the pageant, I spend a little time looking around the vendor booths, watching people, listening to the bands.

Somehow, between the noise and the crowd and my movements through it, I miss her call.

It's not until I'm back in my car, that I see—not only do I have a missed call from Casey, but she left a voicemail.

I'm so happy she called it helps mitigate my disappointment at not hearing from Regan all day.

As I call for my messages, I tell myself, not for the first time, that I need to break things off with Regan and move on. I just can't take her inconsistency and inconsiderateness. I'm not sure what makes her so seemingly schizophrenic, but I've got to have enough self-respect to stop subjecting myself to it.

I punch in my security code and wait.

—Hey, Merrick. It's me.

I can barely hear her over the loud music in the background.

—Can't believe I'm calling you after I was so rude. Sorry about that. I told you I didn't blame you for what happened, but maybe subconsciously I do. I don't know.

She pauses a beat, and I hear a couple of voices yelling above the music like she's at a bar or concert or something—most likely The Dollhouse.

—Anyway, you said to call and I know you meant it—such a good man—it's probably nothing, but there's this guy. Something about him.

Hasn't really done anything yet. I mean sort of, but not really. But he's creeping me out. I'm sure I'm overreacting. It's probably nothing. I'm sure I'm being silly. It's nice to have someone to call. Thanks. Just talking to your voicemail has me feeling better. Like I said, just got a little spooked. I'll call you later. Sorry to be so … I don't know … sensitive or whatever. Okay. Just disregard this whole stupid message. Really. Don't start calling me. Don't freak out. I'll call you in a little while just to let you know I'm fine—which I will be, by the way. Okay. Crazy person signing off now. Love you. Bye.

Against her wishes, I call Casey as I'm driving back into town.

When I get her voicemail, I leave her a message of my own.

—Hey, Case, it's Merrick. Got your message and I was just checking on you. Call me back as soon as you can. Sorry I missed your call, but I'll be listening out now so call again soon. And don't apologize. I'm so glad you called. I *am* here for you. Anything you need. Anytime. Anywhere. You can count on it. I love you.

After ending the call to Casey, I punch in Rashard's number.

—You know where Vic is? I ask.

—I'm not following him or anything, just keeping tabs on him. Why?

—Casey called and said she's being creeped out by some guy and—

—Vic?

—Don't know, I say.

—You didn't ask her?

—It was a voicemail. I'm pretty sure she would've said if it was him. Just wanted to make sure he didn't have anything to do with it.

—I'm not far from 11ᵗʰ, he says. I'll swing by and see if he's home.

—Thanks, man. That'd be great.

—I'll hit you back when I know something.

—Tiffany working tonight?

The big bouncer gives me an elaborate shrug.

Entering The Dollhouse, he's the first person I encounter.

After placing the armband around my wrist, he motions me over to pay the lady behind the counter.

I do.

—Seen Tiffany tonight? I ask her.

She smiles and shakes her head. Sorry, sweetie, but I'm new here, and I can't keep all their little dancer names straight.

She gives me my change, and I place a couple of dollars in her glass tip jar—trying not to think about how few dollars I have left.

—Thanks, sugar, she says. Good luck finding your girl.

It's early—at least in the relative world of a strip club—and the place is busy, but not packed. I normally avoid coming on Friday and Saturday nights because of just how crowded it gets.

I scan the room for Casey, willing myself not to notice if Regan's here or not, the way I had refrained from trying to spot her car in the lot. I'm here for Casey. Wouldn't be otherwise. I'm through chasing a woman who doesn't want to be—or doesn't know what she wants.

It's hard to see everyone in the dim, crowded room—and the flashing stage lights don't help any—but I don't see her.

The remix of "Wicked Games" wraps up, and I take a seat in the front right corner close to the DJ booth and dressing room.

—All right guys, the DJ says, we're setting those two lovely ladies free and bringing up two more. Remember, if you want a private, more personal, intimate dance, all you have to do is ask. Up next, it's Mystic on the main and Sky in the playpen. Mystic on the main, Sky in the pen.

Sitting alone at a strip club is never comfortable, but when it's crowded, when you're surrounded by groups of people laughing, talking, enjoying themselves as they share the experience, it's even more acutely uncomfortable.

Eventually, the waitress makes it over to me, and I'm grateful for someone to interact with and to soon be holding a bottle in my hand.

—What can I get you? she asks, placing a cocktail napkin on the table.

—Corona.

She nods and starts to move away.

—Is Tiffany working tonight?

She purses her lips and looks around.

—Not sure, but I'll find out for you.

—Thanks.

—I thought Raven was your girl.

Shaking my head, I think, Me, too, but I was wrong. She never had been, and I feel myself flush with anger and embarrassment. Do I really mean it this time? Sure. But I did every other time before, too, didn't I?

She leaves, and I look around some more.

Mystic, a tall, thin black girl in a wig, is on her third song on the main, dancing feverishly, cupping her small breasts. The stage is littered with singles, and a group of young black men in baggy outfits that match their baseball caps are standing in front of her, continuing to make it rain.

—Raven, check's out, the DJ says. Raven, check's out.

My pulse quickens at the mention of her name, my body betraying me.

In a moment, I see Regan step out of VIP and head toward the dressing room. Looking away, I'm grateful my beer arrives.

I pay and overtip, and she's about to walk away, but I call her back.

—What about Tiffany? I ask.

—Sorry, she says. I forgot. I'll go find out right now.

—Thanks.

As she walks away, Regan comes up on the other side and attempts to hug me.

—Hey, she says, sitting next to me at the small table. I'm so glad you came in.

—Have you seen Casey?

—No, why?

—Is she working?

—I'm not sure.

The song ends and Sky and Mystic are replaced by Jade and Ling, two Asian dancers, who, with the way they're dressed, could pass for sisters.

—You don't have to cover for her anymore, I say.

—I wasn't covering for her. I just respected her wishes. What's wrong?

—She called and said a guy was bothering her.

—Here? she asks, turning to look around the room.

—She didn't say where she was. Sounded like here.

—I'm surprised she'd call, she says.

—Some people actually do that—make calls, even return calls.

—What's wrong? I meant all she has to do is let a bouncer know.

—Could she be in VIP, not able to let a bouncer know what's going on? I ask.

As soon as I ask it, I realize she was able to call me with her phone. Still, she could've gone in VIP after calling, so we should still check it.

—He walks by at the beginning of every song, but I guess if they were—let me check with the DJ.

She jumps up, disappears into the DJ booth, returning to the table less than a minute later.

—She's not in VIP and she's not on his rotation.

—Meaning? I ask.

—She's not here.

I nod.

—Thanks for checking, I say.

—Are you mad at me?

I shake my head.

—Why're you acting so—

—Any idea where she might be? I ask.

—She's never mentioned going anywhere else. Was she doing something for Thunder Beach?

—Not sure. She wasn't at the Miss Thunder Beach Pageant. I was just out there and didn't see her, but could've easily missed her in the crowd.

I pull out my phone and check it.

—Are you worried about her? she asks.

—Just want to know she's okay.

—Please don't be mad at me.

—I'm not.

—You act like it, she says.

—I do?

—Well, no, you're still polite, but you *are* acting different.

—I'm just here looking for Casey.

—Oh.

—Oh what? I ask.

—I thought … It doesn't matter.

—Doesn't, does it? I say. Took me a while to figure that out.

—What?

The waitress comes back and nods.

—She is, she says.

—What? I ask.

—The girl you asked about. Tiffany. She *is* working tonight.

—You sure?

—Yeah. Diamond and Taylor talked to her.

I turn toward Regan, but she's already up and moving toward the DJ booth.

I stand and begin to walk around the room, winding my way through partying people around small tables, men and women at the tip rails, and girls giving lap dances.

I'm over near the bar when Regan comes up to me.

—She was here earlier, she says, but the DJ thinks she must've left. She didn't tell him, but he called her to the stage several times and she never showed.

—Would you check the dressing room and the girls bathroom?

—Just did. She's not in either of them.

—Nobody saw her leave? I ask.

She shakes her head.

—Not that I've found so far.

—Ask the girl at the desk, I say. I'll check VIP.

—Bouncer won't let you in VIP, she says. Let me do both.

—Okay. Thanks.

I find the waitress, and place a fifty on her tray.

—I'll double that if you can find anyone who saw Tiffany leave and who she left with.

—I'll see what I can do.

Regan comes out of VIP and shakes her head.

We rush over to the front desk.

—You see Tiffany leave? Regan asks.

—Which one is—

I describe Casey.

She nods slowly, seeming to think.

—Yeah.

—When? I ask.

—Why?

Regan puts her hand on my arm.

—It's important, she says. We think she might be mixed up in something.

—Not sure. Hour-and-a-half. Two hours.

—Who'd she leave with?

—She was by herself. Said she didn't feel good. But …

—But what? I ask.

—There was a guy sort of, you know, lingering by the door. I got the feeling he might've been waiting on her.

The manager walks up and stands behind the desk.

—What's going on?

Regan tells him.

—Was she in VIP with the guy before she left? I ask.

The receptionist shrugs.

—I don't know who she was back there with, she says.

—But she was in VIP just before she left?

She nods.

—The rooms have cameras, right? I say.

—Some of them, the manager says, but he's already shaking his head.

—Just let me see who she was with before she left.

—Can't do it. No way. There's no guarantee they were even in a booth with a camera, and even if they were, you can't see much anyway. But I can't let anyone look at that footage. It's part of what we—

—You look at it and describe him to me.

He shakes his head.

—Sorry. Just can't.

I storm out angrily without saying anything—not even to Regan, who can't follow me—and call Rashard as I look around the parking lot.

—You know how hard a search warrant is to get? he asks, after I explain everything to him. No way we get one on what you got.

—*Fuck.*

—Sorry.

—What if you just came and talked to him? Maybe he'd let you watch it.

—He won't. And I can't anyway. This ain't TV. Can't just do whatever in the fuck I want to.

—Yeah. Yeah, I say and end the call.

As I finish searching the parking lot, I try to figure out what to do next.

All the vehicles are empty.

My phone vibrates once to alert me of a voice or text message.

I look at the display. I have a voicemail. Must have come while I was talking to Rashard.

I quickly punch in my security code and listen, my stomach sinking as I do.

—Oh God, Merrick. Where are you? I'm in real trouble.

Distorted, driving music in the background is so loud it's little more than noise makes it nearly impossible to understand her.

—So unbelievably stupid, she is saying. I can't believe that I would be so … over money. I just wanted to be able to stop dancing.

A DJ or an announcer says something, but I can't make it out.

—Anyway, call me as soon as you can or just come to—

There's a struggle.

—No, Casey says. What the fuck—

Somebody yells something.

Casey screams.

The phone is dropped, and a moment later the line is dead.

As I'm about to pull out of The Dollhouse parking lot, Regan runs out and waves me down. She is fully dressed now, a large bag hanging from her shoulder.

I stop and roll down the passenger side window, but she opens the door and gets in.

—I want to help, she says.

—What about your job?

—No longer have it. Said if I left now not to come back. They have to be that way. So many girls try to leave in the middle of their shift—once they've gotten their money.

—Why would you—

—I want to help you.

I pull onto 98, heading west toward the beach, thinking about Regan's actions, wondering what motivates her and why I can't figure it out.

—I don't understand you, I say.

—Whatta you mean?

—You don't return my calls for days at a time, then you quit your job to help me.

—Sorry I couldn't call, but—

—Doesn't matter, I say. Is what it is. But I appreciate your help— and I know Casey will.

—But—

—Finding her is all that matters right now.

My phone vibrates and I see it's Rashard calling me back.

—You get my message? I ask.

—Yeah.

—She's in real trouble. Needs help. What can you do?

—The investigation never stopped, he says. Sheriff Parker talked to Sheriff McKeithan. I know he knows you spoke to her, but until they confirm … Every law enforcement officer in the county's still looking for her. But I'm also gathering some guys I trust for extra help.

Great, I say. Thanks, man. Anyone talk to that Ian King dude?

—Probably not since taking the missing persons report, he says, but I'll find out. Maybe I'll have a go at him.

—Like to be there if you do.

When I end the call, Regan starts to say something, but I immediately call Tristan.

—Ciao, he says.

—Where are you?

—The Curve.

—I need your help.

—No shit?

—None, I say. It's important.

—What's up?

—Can you meet me in the parking lot in about three minutes?

He hesitates a moment.

—I wouldn't ask if it—

—No, it's not that. Sure. I'll be there.

T he parking lot of Newby's Too is filled with rows and rows of bikes. The music of a live band pours out of an open garage door on the end, and patrons spill out of the bar onto the patio, around the picnic tables, and around the Sweet Racks tent.

Unable to find a place to park, I pull up to the entrance where Tristan is waiting, blocking in several bikes as I do.

Jumping out, I cue up Casey's message.

Regan gets out and is standing next to Tristan by the time I get around to them.

—Ciao darlings, he says.

—Tristan, Regan. Regan, Tristan. He's the sickest DJ in town.

—Pleasure, he says, taking and kissing her hand.

—Listen to this, I say, holding the phone up to his ear.

—What am I listening for? … Oh my God. Who's—

—I need to know where she is, I say. Hear the DJ? Is that a DJ or an announcer? What kind of music is that? She left a message earlier tonight. The background noise is very different in this one. She's somewhere else.

—Let me hear it again.

I replay it for him.

If anyone can identify where Casey's calling from, it's Tristan. Not only has he spun records in virtually every venue in the area, he knows all the people involved in that scene.

He presses the phone up to his ear with one hand and covers his opposite ear with the other.

—One more time, he says.

I play it again.

—Where is she? I ask.

He shakes his head, as he squints and looks up, seeming to think about it.

—Not sure, he says. Too distorted. Can probably narrow it down some though. What's going on?

I tell him.

—Shit, man. Okay. Things are a little different this weekend because of the rally. More places have music and bands, but DJ helps narrow it down. Let me think.

—Is it live or canned music? I ask.

—Can't tell. Could be either. In general, there's karaoke at The Backdoor, here at The Curve—except tonight there's a band 'cause of Thunder Beach, and at Sweet Dreams. There's live music at Mrs. Newbys, Dysfunction Junction, La Vela, Spinaker, Sharky's, Hammerhead Fred's, Club Oxygen, Tootsies, The Tiki Bar, and maybe Latitudes.

—But they wouldn't have DJs, right? I say.

—Right. May have announcers, though.

—Then there's Splash, the gay bar out here. Probably doesn't have a band, but will be playing dance music and probably have an announcer.

—So many possibilities, I say.

—More this weekend than usual. In town, there's also the strip clubs—Tan Fannies, Gold Nugget, Toy Box, and The Dollhouse. There's a small joint over in Springfield, Bambi's Dollhouse or something, but don't think it has a DJ.

—Tan Fannies doesn't have a DJ, I say.

—Oh, that's right, he says. There's also The Fiesta—the gay bar downtown. There could be other places I don't know about—or, you know, that're doing something special just for this weekend. Rarely do places have a DJ with a live band, but for the rally … I don't know. I bet some have local radio personalities—Kramer, Holly, Miguel, 6-Pack, Dr. Shane, some of those guys. I'll make a few calls and find out.

—Just give me most likely, I say.

He thinks about it for another moment.

—Lot of pressure, he says. Don't want to lead you astray.

—We gotta start somewhere. You're our best bet.

—La Vela, Spinaker, The Dollhouse, Nugget, Toy Box, Splash, Oxygen, Fiesta—oh, and Stetson's.

—The country place?

—Used to be. It's changed. They have a DJ and a band. The others are possibilities, but longer shots. You got a picture of her?

—Yeah. Why?

—We could split up. I could take a few.

—You don't mind?

—Happy to, he says. She's hot.

The drive out to Spinaker and La Vela is slow, and I try calling Casey periodically.

—I'm sorry I did it again, Regan says.

—What?

—Withdrew.

I nod.

—I'm so unhappy with Gabe, but … He's unhappy, too. Not just unhappy—that sounds so juvenile. We're in different places, going in different directions, but I feel so sorry for him. Our relationship is over, run its course, but we've shared—not just a life together, but losing …

She drifts off and I know she means Tina, their daughter who died.

—I'm having a hard time leaving him, she adds.

—I'm not asking you to.

—What?

—It's taken a while, but I get it. And I understand. I do.

—But—

—We'll find Casey, put all this behind us, and be friends.

—Friends?

—Yeah. I meant it when I said I loved you. I'll be here for you. Always. You can count on that. Do anything I can for you. I'm sorry if I put pressure on you or wasn't understanding enough. Like you said, we're heading in two different directions.

—I said that about me and Gabe.

—Oh. Well … it applies.

—So, what, you don't want me anymore?

—That was never our problem.

—But it is now?

—No. It's not a problem.

—But you don't want me? she says.

—I'm not letting myself. Desire doesn't go away—at least not for me, not that fast.

—So we're … what? Through? Just like that?

—Not through. No. I told you, I'll be a great friend if you'll let me. I'm just stopping the cycle.

—What happened?

I think about it.

—You know what I think it is? I say. I think the pattern just re-peated itself one too many times.

—I can't believe this. You're punishing me for having a hard time letting go of my marriage?

—You think I'm punishing you?

—What it feels like.

—It's not that at all.

—Then what? she asks.

—I've already said.

—My marriage will end anyway. It's just a matter of when.

—Then our timing was bad.

The enormous parking lot at La Vela is full of semi trailers, vendor tents, and motorcycles. There are a few people wandering around, but obviously most are inside the club.

The elaborately painted tractor trailers have murals of brands and products I recognize—from motorcycle companies to energy drinks— but the two that stick out the most are one for a traveling tattoo parlor, the sides of which have a fully nude, heavily inked and pierced young woman lying on her side, stretching the full length of the trailer, and an all black trailer with simple white letters that reads Pure Pleasure Massage and Escort Services.

—Can't find a date to take to Thunder Beach, Regan says, buy one when you get here. Pay a little extra and get a happy ending.

I'm about to say something when Tristan calls.

—Ciao baby, he says. Forgot to tell you. Go to Spit On Her first.

—Come again.

—Spit On Her—it's what we call Spinaker. Spinaker is Spit On Her and La Vela is Velveeta. Go to Spinaker first and tell them you work with Chris over at Pizza Hut. Should get you in. Then go to the PFM tent in front of La Vela. Tell 6-Pack I sent you. He'll get you in. If he's not there, look for Larry Gordan.

—Cool. Thanks, man.

—All part of the service.

Located right next to La Vela, Spinaker is part club, part restaurant, and caters to a slightly older demographic.

Tonight it's quiet.

Of course, it's still early—and most people are probably at the concert next door—but I don't think Casey called from here.

The Gulfside Rock Arena is mostly empty—a few girls gathered around the bar, two couples at a table upstairs, a lone guitarist strumming a Jimmy Buffet tune on stage. Along the backside next to the beach, the Paradise Grill is filled with families eating hamburgers.

We pause for a moment on the top deck and look out over Thomas Drive and the east end of the beach. Across the street, beyond the bikes and vendors, beyond the traffic and pedestrians and bar patrons, kids scream as they're propelled over ten stories into the air between the two giant red-lit arms of the bungee Slingshot.

We take a quick stroll through the Groove Room and the VIP Lounge, but both are quiet, the partying not having started yet.

I'm so certain she didn't call from here, I don't even pull out her picture and pass it around.

Billed as the largest nightclub in the US, La Vela is a mammoth, multi-venue facility with several parties occurring simultaneously in theme rooms. Each with its own vibe and ambiance, the rooms cater to different tastes.

Tonight the concert coliseum on the west end of the pool deck is packed with people listening to a Lynyrd Skynyrd tribute band. As we walk in, they're covering one of my favorite Skynyrd songs, "Simple Man," thousands of fans in front of and around the lagoon-shaped pool swaying and singing along.

We stand on the elevated area not far from the entrance and look around.

People continue to pour in through the gates—bikers in jeans and leather, college-age guys in plaid shorts and T-shirts, young women in party dresses and high heels.

Not sure where to start, I'm overwhelmed by all the various rooms—Thunderdome, Night Gallery, Underground, Rock Arena, Pussy Kat Lounge, Foam, Galaxy, Space, Dark Room, and Posh Ultra Lounge.

We turn away from the concert and make our way up toward the entrances to the other clubs.

—Should we split up? Regan asks.

I shrug.

—Probably not a bad idea.

—Okay, she says. Call me.

—You gonna answer if I do? I ask with a smile.

We aren't apart for long.

Every room at La Vela is closed until after the concert except Thunderdome.

—The gods are smiling on us, she says. We could've spent all night just at just this one place.

We walk up the incline and into the largest of the clubs in the complex, and the moment I hear the music and DJ coming through the 75,000 watt sound system I know this could very well be where Casey called from.

Daric "The Hitman" Daniels is spinning dance remixes of top 40 songs in the elevated booth to the right of the giant, black, backlit V, as hundreds of people dance beneath the enormous disco ball and massive hanging truss system of rotating lights and moving cryogenics.

Regan looks at me, and I nod.

We both withdraw the folded cover photos of Casey we're carrying and get to work.

—I'll take the first bar, she says, pointing toward the area to our left and closest to the entrance.

—I'll take those I say, indicating the two other bars—one in the center, one along the far wall.

As I move further in, I call Tristan. I get his voicemail.

—See if this sounds like Casey's message, I shout into the phone, telling him I'll do this at each place we go to. Text me back. No way I'll be able to hear you in here.

The female bartender at the center setup is the busiest in the building, but takes the time to look at the picture and pass it around to a few of the patrons who've been sitting there the longest. None of them have seen Casey.

I move around the large room, looking, scanning, searching for her blond hair.

In contrast to the adult biker crowd outside around the pool for the concert, those gathered here skew much younger—older teens and twenty-somethings—all dolled up and on the make. Singles. Couples. Girls running in small packs.

I show the picture to anyone willing to look at it—and a few people who aren't, but I get the same response—the shake of a head or a yelled, No, sorry, from the girls, and a, No man, ain't seen her, from the guys.

By the time Regan and I have gotten back together, Tristan has texted to say he's fairly certain she didn't call from here and that he struck out at Sweet Dreams and Sharky's.

Crossing Thomas Drive on foot, we enter Dysfunction Junction, through the bar in the front to the concert venue in the back. There's a band, but no DJ.

We hang around for a few moments to see if the lead singer says anything above the music that sounds like a DJ, but he doesn't. Just in case, I call Tristan again and leave him a message.

With Tristan checking Club Oxygen and Mrs. Newby's, Regan and I head back into town to hit The Toy Box, The Gold Nugget, Stetson's, and The Fiesta.

—I appreciate your help, I say, but I can drop you at your car if you like.

—What? she asks.

—I can drop you off so you can get on home. Think I can handle it from here.

—You do, do you? You can go into the girls' bathrooms and the strippers' dressing rooms?

I laugh.

—Guess not, I say.

—Why you in such a hurry to get rid of me? she asks.

—I'm not. I just—

—Come on, she says. You're through with me and you know it. *I repeated the pattern one too many times.*

—I'm not through with you. I told you.

—Yeah. Yeah. You'd do anything you can for me.

—I will.

—How can you just cut your feelings off?

—I haven't. And I'm not playing games. I've noticed before when I'd back off like you seemed to want, you'd start pursuing me. I'm not trying to get you to do that. I swear.

—I can tell. I want to tell you a story.

—Has it got a wow finish? I ask, thinking of Rick sitting in his dark saloon, drunk as fuck, Ilsa standing before him.

—What? she asks, confused.

—Just a line from Casablanca.

—Oh. It's about a girl who met a man in a strip club once.

—Yeah, I say, I've heard a lot of stories like this. They all start the same. Mister, I met a man once in a strip club.

—Can I tell my story? She's a stripper with barely an AA degree, and he's a reporter and a professor and they're an unlikely pair, but he shows her real love.

—Sounds like a great guy, I say.

—He is. And she really responds to him, but she also gets freaked out. I mean, she's in a relationship that's dead, but not in the ground yet. And the truth is, she's damaged goods—has been since … since she … lost her daughter, and always will be. But he seems to understand that, too. Anyway, so she retreats sometimes, gets so close to the flame of his love she thinks she'll be consumed by it, and she runs. But she gets past that. She does. And then she loses her phone. And he thinks she's doing it again—and who can blame him—but she's not. She's really ready to move forward with him and he says he just wants to be friends.

I'm not quite sure what to say, and so drive in silence for a while.

We ascend the flyover ramp, only the tops of pine trees, a high-rise, and a few random billboards visible above the short concrete walls. As we crest the Hathaway Bridge, lights from the Port of Panama City shimmer in the dark waters of the bay on the right, the lit buildings of the college rising up out of the campus on the left.

—You not gonna respond? she asks finally.

—I'm sorry.

—For what?

—Everything, but mostly at the moment for the loss of your daughter.

She sniffles in the darkness and I can tell she's tearing up.

We come to The Toy Box first.

It's a small strip club with a stage in the front and bar in the back. Actually, I should probably call it an exotic dancer club because, as one of the girls explained to me, she's not a stripper because she doesn't strip off *all* her clothes.

The DJ booth is high against the right wall, towering over the open private dance room—if you want a lap dance here, you have to get it in a room with other people getting theirs.

The place is dim, lit mostly by the glow of neon and rope lights, the music is loud, but not nearly so as the other places we've been to.

Regan and I enter separately. I take a seat at a small table near the stage. She poses as a dancer and checks the women's restroom and the dancers' dressing room.

I order a Corona from the waitress, then tip the dancer on stage. By the time my beer arrives, the dancer is sitting next to me.

A single mom from Alabama, Candy barely opens her mouth when she speaks, which only serves to accentuate her severe southern drawl. Beneath her white sheer lingerie, the only thing about her that looks like she had a baby just over a month ago are her breasts.

We talk for a while, which is pleasant except for the fact that she's a chain smoker and we're in very close proximity. Her speech and movements are so slow, her words so soft and hard to understand, I wonder if she's on something, or drunk, or slow, or just sleep deprived, and decide, it's likely a combination of all the above.

The DJ has a wireless microphone and is out of the booth as much as he's in it—up and down the stairs, in and out the door—and when he's announcing I call Tristan and leave a message to see if it sounds like the one Casey left.

—Wanna a lap dance? Candy asks.

—Would love one, but actually don't have time. I'll pay you for two just to answer one question for me.

I pull out two twenties and the folded picture of Casey.

—Has she been in tonight?

—Why you lookin' for her?

I tell her.

She picks up the glossy magazine cover and holds it close to her face, straining to see in the dim room, and studies it for a long moment.

Over by the bar in the back, one of the dancers shoots pool with a customer, her T-back thong and skimpy bra making the activity look more odd than sexy.

Eventually, Candy shakes her head.

—She looks familiar, she says, but I don't think I've ever seen her in here.

—You're sure?

She nods.

—And you don't have to pay me for that, she says.

—I want to, I say, sliding the twenties across the table to her.

—Thanks, she says, folding them into her garter with the rest of her stash.

—How long you been here tonight? Anybody else I should ask?

—I've been here all night, but we can ask Andy, just in case I missed her.

She stands and walks back to the bouncer, a young, bald, white man with a thick, bushy goatee, sitting behind the reception counter. Greeter, cashier, and bouncer, Andy is soft spoken and gentle.

He shakes his head after looking at the cover.

—She ain't been in, he says. Not since I've been here.

Regan walks up.

—You decide not to dance? Andy asks.

—Yeah. Just got my period and have a horrible headache.

He nods.

—Another time, she says, and walks out.

—Well, thanks for your help, I say, dropping my card on the counter. If she does come in, will you give me a call?

—Sure thing, he says. No problem.

In the parking lot, beneath the giant lighted Maharaja's billboard, Regan and I pause before getting in the car.

—She wasn't in there and hasn't been in.

—Thanks for doing that.

—Probably wind up working here after walking out of The Dollhouse.

Stetson's is not what I expect at all.

The décor is strictly country/western, but everything else is club.

On our way over, we had stopped by The Gold Nugget, but with the assistance of the manager, the bouncer, and a particularly cute and helpful shooter girl, quickly determined Casey had not been there.

When we arrive, the band is on a break, and the whitest sounding black DJ I've ever heard yells into a microphone that's already turned up too high, and plays dance music so loud I think it might actually rupture my eardrums.

The large venue is packed, and the crowd is far more diverse than I imagined—black and white, young and old, dance and drink and dialog—especially for what I thought was a redneck joint.

Middle-aged white men in cowboy hats standing next to young black men in hip-hop attire watch as fifty-something females shake their groove things alongside twenty-somethings on the dance floor.

I look over at Regan.

—This what you expected?

She shakes her head and smiles.

—I figured we were walking into a place out of *Urban Cowboy.*

—This is amazing. Even if it weren't a country joint, I wouldn't expect to see such a wide range of people.

—Everybody wants to party, she says. Why not do it together?

—They just rarely do.

On the dance floor, a young girl wearing a crown celebrates her bachelorette party with her friends, as everyone cheers.

—She's just a child, I say.

—She's a rebel.

—How you figure?

—Trend is to marry later these days, she says.

—Not around here, I bet.

—Here?

—I guess I meant the Deep South.

She twists her lips into a sad smirk and nods.

As I move through the room, and Regan checks the girls' bathroom, I call Tristan and leave a message while the music is playing and the DJ is talking.

It takes a while to get through the crowd and to pass the photo around, but when we're finished, we're both convinced she hasn't been here—ever.

Just as diverse, but less surprising, is Panama City's only gay bar, The Fiesta/ La Royale Lounge.

It's less surprising because when you're the only gay bar around, it stands to reason you'll attract gay people of all ages and races. What I hadn't counted on was how many heterosexual people the place drew, but I soon discover why.

As if transplanted from the French Quarter in New Orleans, the old brick buildings are joined by an enclosed courtyard, The Fiesta on one side, La Royale Lounge on the other.

We park on Harrison right off Beach Drive, but can't get in from here.

—Gay bar, Regan says. Have to enter in rear.

I shake my head.

—Come on, she says. I know it's an old and bad joke, but it'll probably be the only time in my life I'll ever get to use it.

We arrive just before the first of three drag shows of the night. Beneath a large disco ball, several couples and a few individuals dance on a low stage.

The couples are comprised of men and women, women and women, and men and men, and it's a beautiful thing.

As the dance music fades, a slow song comes on and even more people crowd onto the small stage. Of all the couples, the two most striking are a young man with cerebral palsy dancing with one of the waitresses and two giant, muscular, masculine men dancing with each other.

—Wish we had time to take a twirl, I say. 'Cause I'd like to be part of that.

She stops and looks at me, a warm, appreciative smile on her face.

—What?

—I love you, she says.

We stand there a long moment, staring at each other, tiny dots of light dancing across our bodies. It's magic, even transcendent, and everything else in the world seems to dim and fade away.

Eventually, we embrace, pressing our bodies so hard against each other, it's more like clinging than hugging.

The song ends, and we let go.

—Come on, she says. Let's find Casey so we can figure out what to do about the fact that we both love each other.

While Regan checks the girls bathroom and the crowd in The Fiesta, I walk to the bar in the back where the two bartenders are dancing and dry humping each other as they work.

At the end of the bar closest to me, three ladies from the drag show discuss their upcoming performances.

—Hell-ooo handsome, the tall African-American in a black evening dress says. She is standing. I'm a little over six feet, and I have to look up at her.

 —Ladies, I say.

 —Wanna buy a girl a drink? the thin blonde seated at the bar says.

 —That's exactly what I want to do.

 I motion the bartender.

 —Another of whatever these three girls are having—and give me the gayest drink you can make.

 —You got it, sweetheart, he says.

 It's the first time a guy has ever called me sweetheart.

 —What *is* the gayest drink they make? I ask.

 The three ladies think about it.

 —Sour apple martini.

 —Sea breeze.

 —Depends on who's drinking it, darling. If it's a dyke, the gayest drink will be the butchest, if a fag, then the most froufrou.

 I nod, and we're quiet for a moment.

 Over near the stage, those seated at the small bar tables have an eerie milky glow from the black lights above them.

 —I'm looking for a girl, I say.

 —Came to the right place, honey, the most masculine of the three says in a deep voice.

 She's in a black bodysuit, fishnets, high heels, with a white shirt tied up beneath her enormous breasts.

 —Obviously, I say.

 I pull out the picture of Casey and pass it around.

 When all the responses are negative, I pay for the drinks, take mine—little umbrella, erect banana and all—and step out into the courtyard.

 The brick courtyard is filled with plants and patio tables beneath the night sky and the looming white elephant of St. Andrews Tours.

At the small bar, I repeat the routine from inside—and get the same results.

More a traditional bar, La Royale Lounge has a jukebox, a pool table, and a long bar that runs the length of the inside wall—bottles of liquor for sale lined up behind it.

Up on the bar top, two boys in nothing but their underwear and socks dance as patrons look up lustfully.

Like The Fiesta, everyone in La Royale Lounge is friendly and welcoming—and the young, male bartender calls me sugar. Again, a first.

Regan joins me, and I pass the picture around while she checks the bathroom.

No joy.

As we make our way back through the courtyard and through The Fiesta, the show has started.

On stage, a female impersonator lip syncs to "I Wanna be Bad," as patrons clap and cheer from their seats, while others stand at the edge of the stage with singles to tip—receiving a kiss on the cheek for their kindness.

—Wish we could stay, I say.

—We'll come back, she says.

I smile as I'm filled with a warmth that emanates from what seems the very center of me, but my smile fades and something cold instantly replaces the heat when she thoughtlessly, recklessly adds another preposterous promise.

—We'll do everything, she says. Everything.

—**H**ey, faggot.

We've only taken a few steps down the sidewalk on our way back to the car.

I turn toward the angry voice, a physiological change already taking place inside me—pulse quickening, respiration increasing, adrenaline spiking.

As I spin around, I sweep Regan behind me with one arm, bringing the other up defensively.

—Knew who I was talkin' to, didn't he?

The two men stepping out of the shadows have shaved heads that gleam ghostly white in the night. They carry aluminum baseball bats.

—Knew who I was talkin' to, didn't you, faggot?

This comes from the younger of the two—an early twenties, stocky white man with icy blue eyes.

Next to him, the mid-fifties man, who is taller and bigger and softer, is dressed identically, as if flannel shirts, camo fatigues, and black boots constitute a uniform.

—You like it the ass, don't you, faggot? You sick piece of shit. See how you like it when I jam my big Louisville Slugger up your shitter.

—What's with the cunt? the older one says, shifting his glazed-eye glare onto Regan. She a chick with a dick or a fuckin' muff divin' dyke?

—Your tits real, freak? the younger one asks her.

With their attention directed toward Regan, I try to figure out a move.

They have us cornered against a tall brick wall. If it were just me, it'd be difficult enough to get away, but with Regan, grabbing her hand and running is not an option. Of course, fighting two men with bats isn't much of one either.

—You gotta shriveled up little dick in your panties, darlin'? You wanna be a girl so goddam bad, I'll cut it off for you. How 'bout that?

Huh?

I think about the love and acceptance we had just witnessed inside, the experience the environment had inspired, the way Regan had been moved to tell me she loved me, and its contrast with the surreal world we've walked into—the fear, ignorance, brutality, and hate these men embody.

Someone like these remorseless men before me had Casey, and if they hospitalize or kill us, I'll never be able to find her, to save her, to make up for abandoning her, to prove to her that she can count on me, that I'll always come for her.

But what can I do?

How can I possibly protect Regan and prevent what, at the moment, seems unstoppable, certain, inevitable?

The more I think about the situation, the more I'm convinced the best I can hope to do is tackle the men so Regan can run for help. But will she? If I lunge into them, knock them both down, accept the brutal beating in the fight that follows, will she run or freeze? Will she see the opportunity to run as a chance to secure help or an act of abandonment?

I'll know soon enough.

—I don't know, the younger one is saying. These two sure are pretty. Maybe we should take them home so we can take our time.

—There's an idea, the older one says. Maybe we—

Placing my foot on the brick wall behind us, I push off, diving toward the men, as if on a football field, arms spread out, knocking them down.

We crash to the pavement, bats clanging, rolling, coming to rest on the curb a few feet away.

—RUN, I yell.

Regan doesn't move.

—Hurry. Get help.

She turns to run, as I struggle to hold the two men down.

As we scramble around, all three of us reaching for the bats, I glance over to see she is gone.

I reach the bats first, but as I attempt to grab one, the men grip my ankles and jerk me back, scraping my stomach and chest on the asphalt.

Flipping over, I begin to kick at the men and try to crab crawl away.

As the older one holds me, the younger jumps up and runs over and grabs one of the bats.

Kicking my way to freedom, I spin around toward the man with the bat, lifting my hands in a futile attempt to protect myself from the imminent attack, while simultaneously trying to roll away.

—HEY.

The yell comes from behind the man with the bat.

He turns to see the Fiesta's bouncer standing there.

We all freeze.

The bouncer is a slightly overweight, middle-aged man with thinning white hair and glasses. Wearing a pink T-shirt, jeans, and bright white tennis shoes, there's nothing imposing or threatening about him.

—Hey yourself, you cock-suckin' faggot. You're just in time to have a bat shoved up your ass, too.

Regan appears a few feet behind the bouncer, and I push myself up off the ground.

As the young man lifts the bat in preparation to swing, the bouncer snaps out a short, stiff right hand jab, breaking the guy's nose.

He drops the bat and the bouncer catches it before it hits the ground.

With the man holding his bloody nose, the bouncer grips the bat, pulls it back, and swings it into the man's abdomen.

As the man falls to the ground, unable to catch his breath, the bouncer pounces on the other man—hitting him in the back of the knees, causing him to crumple, then driving a hard thwack into his back.

Neither man attempts to get up.

—I suck cock and I can kick your ass, the bouncer says.

—A man of many talents, I say.

—You two okay? He asks, turning toward us.

We nod.

—Nazi motherfuckers wait out here occasionally to do some literal gay bashing.

—Thank you, I say. You saved our—

—What I'm here for. I'm gonna call the cops. If you don't want to get tangled up in this, you can go ahead and get out of here.

—Thanks, I say, wanting to apologize to him for a world with people like these men in it, but not knowing how to exactly.

—Last few years, the beach has really changed, Tristan is saying. There's an edge, a danger that used not to be here.

We are in the parking lot of The Dollhouse waiting for Brad, Stephen, and Kyle.

Regan nods like she really knows what he means.

—More bad shit happenin'. I'm not talkin' partyin'. I'm talkin' crime. People getting' seriously fucked—robbed, raped, beaten, killed.

He's not the first person to say this, and though I haven't experienced very much in the way of violence or violation firsthand, I have interviewed a number of people who have.

—You heard about the hotel security guy who raped the girl last summer and threw her body off the balcony to make it look like she fell, he continues. And there's just a lot of freaky shit—some wacky, wacky stuff.

Having turned up not a single sighting during our search of clubs with DJs, we've met here because I have an idea for how to find out who Casey left with.

Brad arrives, followed shortly by Stephen and Kyle.

We huddle.

—Desperate times, I say. But what we're about to attempt is illegal. If it works, it'll get some of us in trouble. If it doesn't, it'll get all of us in trouble. If you don't want to be involved, no one'll hold it against you.

—I fuckin' live for fuckin' trouble, Brad says.

—He didn't get the name Brad to the Bone for teaching Sunday School, Tristan says.

—Fuck it, Stephen says. I'm in.

—Me, too, Kyle adds.

—You can both count on A's in my class—even if you don't show up for the rest of the semester.

—It's our favorite class, Kyle says. We'll be there.

—When you get out of jail, I say.

—The plan involves us going to jail? Stephen asks.

I nod.

—Let's hear it.

—A while back when I was here, a fight broke out, and everybody scrambled. You two guys will pick a fight—just don't involve any of the girls. Start something with a customer—someone big enough to take care of himself. Make it big and sloppy and involve as many people as you can. When the bouncers come, Brad will interfere—a fellow bouncer trying to help, but really prolonging it—try to get the manger going, too. While this is happening, Regan will distract the woman behind the counter, and Tristan and I will sneak into the office and look at the surveillance footage from earlier tonight.

—You're not gonna have very long inside the office, Brad says.

—I know. But I've got the time of her call, so I should be able to zip back to it pretty fast. They'll take you guys outside and wait on the cops—unless you can talk them into not making that call. Either way, we should be able to get what we need.

—I've got a snub nose .38 in my car, Brad says. In case you—

—No guns, I say. If we're caught it changes everything.

He nods.

I look around.

—Any questions?

—The one time I saw the entire club empty out, Regan says, was when somebody sprayed mace. I have some in the car.

Brad nods.

—I'll take it and use it if we need a Plan B.

As if part of an artistic action film, the beat of the techno dance music and the flashing lights give the fight a heightened, surreal aspect that makes it look choreographed.

Tables turn, chairs fly, strippers scatter.

The poor guy they pick the fight with is a squat, muscular man who continually flexes and strikes competition-type poses whether at the tip rail or standing next to his table of friends.

Coming in about two minutes after we're in position, and just before the fight starts, Regan creates drama by claiming she's owed money by the house—ensuring Tristan and I are able to slip into the office unseen, and she will never work here again.

Down a short, narrow hallway, last office on the right, and we're looking at a computer-based security monitoring system.

With Tristan at the door, watching the hallway, I use the mouse to navigate to about the time of Casey's first call and work back from there.

Because there are ten feeds, which include seven of the ten VIP rooms, one on the reception counter, and one on the entrance, each window is small, and it takes me a while to locate her.

Once I have, I increase the size of the window displaying her and a trim, dark haired man with a Caesar cut.

It's difficult for me to see her bare breasts and seductive dance, but know I can't look away for even a moment.

Freezing the frame with the best possible view of the man, I pull out my phone and take a picture of the screen.

Continuing forward, I lose her as they leave the room, but pick her up a few minutes later at the reception counter, preparing to leave. As she talks to the woman behind the desk, Caesar stands by the entrance waiting for her.

I'm snapping a few more pics of the screen when the door at the end of the hallway opens, smoke and music pouring in with it, and Tristan begins to shake and stammer.

—Isssss … it …. over? Is it over? he asks.

—The fuck you doin' back here?

—Hiding, man. Got scared.

I slip right behind him and pretend to be hiding, too.

It's the smaller of the two bouncers, a white guy with a shaved head, goatee, and a massive dangling earring, and I think how curious it is that most of the guys working the doors around town sport this same style.

—We can't be anywhere close to a fight, I say. We violate our probation and we go down for a deuce. Hundred bucks if you can sneak us out of here without anyone seeing.

He hesitates.

—Two hundred, Tristan says.

—Follow me, he says.

He leads us to a hidden door in the next office, and we come out on the side of the building next to the air conditioning units.

I hand him a hundred dollar bill.

He looks at Tristan.

—He's got mine, too, Tristan says.

—I would, I say, but I don't have it. I'll pay you back.

I'm getting down to the last of the cash I had and the very last of little money I've been living on lately.

—Would you take sixty and a Walmart gift card? Tristan asks.

The bouncer growls.

—I've got forty, I say, and hand it to Tristan, who puts my two twenties with his three, and then places them in the open, waiting palm of the big man.

By the time Tristan and I make it to our cars, Regan is there waiting on us.

—How'd it go? I ask.

—Everyone did a great job, but all three of them are going to jail.

—Shit.

—It's cool, Tristan says. I'll go get them out.

—I'll hit up an ATM, I say, pay you back and send bail money with you.

I'm pretty sure I don't have enough in my account to cover everything, but I'll have to figure out what to do about that tomorrow. Right now, with Casey in danger and the merciless clock ticking, my inability to fund this little operation is the least of my concerns.

—Get what you needed? Regan asks.

I nod.

—Ever seen this guy? I ask, holding up the phone.

—Yeah, she says, on an Ancient Roman coin.

—Where can we clean this up and print it out? I ask.

—I know a place, Tristan says. I'll take you. It'll be a while before Brad and the boys will be processed.

I look at the image on the small screen.

—Wait 'til I get my hands on this motherfucker.

Hippie Dave, a tall, aging radical with a long gray ponytail and full, flowing white beard, lives in the Cove and runs a cultural, political, and literary zine out of his garage. He's a big man with thick hands, long fingernails, and small, but intense hazel eyes behind black frame glasses, the corners of which are held together with electrical tape.

He's a friend of Tristan's, and is more than willing to help, but moves slowly and seems completely baked as he attempts to negotiate the stacked boxes and piled papers filling the garage.

It takes far longer than I would've liked for him to print the picture and to create and copy the flyers, and the entire time, my heart and head are pounding, anxiety jangling through my nerves like lightning.

I move around constantly, bumping into cardboard boxes, tripping over stacks of newspapers and back issues of Hippie Dave's zines, my mind repeating the mantra, I've gotta find her. I've gotta find her. I've gotta find her.

It's all I can think about. I keep picturing her with the creep from the club with the Caesar cut. She's out there somewhere, and he's got her. I've got to find her before it's too late.

By the time we have the flyers made, and Regan and I are racing back out to the beach to pass them out, Rashard calls.

—Where are you? he asks.

—Back Beach, I say. Close to Ed's Sheds.

—Pull over.

I do, dread filling me, as if a dark, powerful poison pumped into me intravenously is now coursing through every cell of blood in my body.

—What is it? Regan asks.

—Who's with you?

—Regan. Why?

—Let me speak to her.

—No.

—What is it? Just tell me.

—Merrick, listen to me. Just—

—No. I can't. Just … Don't. Please … Please tell me she's not …

Regan leans up in her seat and looks over at me, her face tortured and contorted.

—Prepare yourself, he says.

There's no way to, and we both know it.

—What? What is it? I ask, but I know, and yet I don't want to know, don't want to hear him say it.

Images of Casey flash in my mind. In only a few moments, I picture little Casey in Disney Princesses' costumes, her long, blond hair held up in a homemade bow; as a gawky, preteen with a boy's body in jeans and an oversized rock T-shirt; as a stunning young woman in a burgundy prom dress, the only sign of the girl she had been her kind, innocent, bright blue eyes. She had been eleven when I started seeing her mom, so some of the memories come from photographs and old videos, but they're no less real, and it feels as if I were always there, always her dad;

her, always my daughter.

—We found her.

—Wait. No. Just wait a minute.

Cars and trucks and motorcycles slash by, streaks of light in the night.

—I'm so sorry, man, he says, and I can hear in his voice just how true his statement is.

Now the image of Casey in my mind is that of a victim. Raped. Murdered. Dumped. Nothing he can tell me, nothing I can see could be as bad as what I'm imagining.

—She's … He … We found her … She's dead.

—No, I yell, getting out of the car, pacing along the shoulder, no concern for the heavy flow of traffic whizzing by.

Regan gets out of the car, staying close by, but not right next to me.

—She can't be, I say.

—I'm sorry.

—How? Where?

—We won't know for a while, but it looks like an overdose.

—Where are you? I want to see her.

—I'm sorry, man, but you can't, he says. Get Regan to take you home. When I know more, I'll give you a call. I promise.

—Don't do that, I say. I need to be there. I've got to … She needs someone to …

—I know, but … you just can't. You know that.

—Goddammit, Rashard. Tell me where you are.

—What is it? Regan asks.

I shake my head and wave her away.

—I just can't, he says. You know that—or should. You'll understand one day. Even if I did, detectives wouldn't let you within a mile of their crime scene. But even if they would, you don't need to see this, don't need to see her. Not like this.

He paused for a moment, but I don't say anything. I can't.

—I've got to go, he says. I'm so, so sorry. I wish … I just don't know what to say. I'll take care of everything on this end—look out for her, guard her dignity. I promise. I'll call you tomorrow. We can talk then. Just be careful tonight. Don't do anything reckless. Go home, try to rest and get yourself together. I'll know more tomorrow. I'll get with you then. I've got to go.

He ends the call, and I stumble through telling Regan.

—Oh God, Merrick, she says, pulling me into a hug, holding me for a long moment.

Behind us, beyond the chain link fence, the storage units stand still and silent in the dark, damp, night air.

I don't cry—and I'm not sure why. Probably partly out of shock, partly out of fatigue, and partly because somewhere deep inside, in some dark corner, a part of me had expected this, had believed this to be the inevitable end of this nightmare.

—I'm gonna find the man who did it and kill him, I say.

Regan nods, not in agreement, but understanding.

We are back in my car, still parked in front of Ed's—unable to stand any longer, unsure about what to do next.

—I'll have to take care of Kevin, I say. I've got to find him. He has no one now. I didn't mean *have* to. I *want* to.

—I know, she says.

—It's gonna be a big job. You might want to run now—while you still can. Probably won't want to be around for whatever the fuck this is we're doing.

—I'm not going anywhere.

She says it with such matter-of-fact certitude, that I almost believe her—this, in spite of her history, of the way she has vanished after intimate moments just like this one.

—I know what you're thinking, she says, but I mean it. You'll see. My decision's made. Before, I was trying to make it. Everything's different now.

I don't say anything, just give a small nod, but I'm not sure she sees it.

We are quiet a moment, and in the silence, my many failures where Casey's concerned haunt me, and I begin to shake.

—What is it? Regan asks.

—Just can't believe I failed her again.

—You didn't.

—It's all I ever done—let her down, abandon her, fuck up her life.

She shakes her head.

—There's no way that's true, she says. I know you. I know the kind of—

—It is.

—How?

I think about it, not sure I really want to get into it.

—You married their mom? she asks.

I nod.

—So you were their dad for a while?

—Not legally. Perry—their bio dad would never have gone for that, but I felt like their dad. We were really, really close. Especially me and Case. Perry wasn't involved much at all—an occasional phone call, birthday and Christmas gifts, that was about it. Mainly because of Kevin.

—Her younger brother?

—Yeah.

—Why?

—He has autism. I think their father was close to Casey before Kevin was born, but began to pull away from them both. Casey was very protective over Kevin. If her dad didn't want to see them both, he wouldn't get to see either of them.

I think about all the things Casey, Kevin, and I used to do together—the hours at the park, at the beach, our late-night trips to eat or bowl or to a midnight movie, Monica back at home, asleep in her bed.

—What happened? she asks.

I frown and shake my head.

—Monica and I were so unhappy. I'm talking major league miserable.

—You … she says, and shakes her head, studying me intently.

—What?

—You stayed with her because of kids that weren't even yours.

I shrug.

—They were mine.

She nods.

—Eventually, we had a child together. Ty.

—Which meant a man like you would *never* leave.

—A man like me?

I let out a small humorless laugh.

—I know men, she says. Seen all kinds. Heard everything. Every single week at the club I hear the lines and lies of a hundred guys. I know. Trust me. You're a good man. Got what so many are lacking—character. I see how you are. You wouldn't leave those kids.

—I couldn't, I say.

—So what happened? You never told me how it . . .

—Monica was bringing Ty back from a doctor's appointment. It was raining. Hard. The roads were … so wet. She had the cruise control on … and hit a huge pool of water on the road … she … hydroplaned, lost control, but the tires kept spinning at fifty-something miles an hour. The car flipped, rolled a few times, crashed through a guardrail, and sank into the Dead Lakes. She was probably dead from the impact before the car went into the … water … but …

I feel myself starting to breakdown, and pause a moment to take a breath.

—With his mom unconscious behind the wheel, Ty sat trapped in his carseat as the dark water that would kill him rose around him.

—Oh, God, Merrick, I'm so, so sorry. I …

Her words contain the genuine empathy of a mother who's lost a child, and she now knows more fully why I understood her loss the way I do.

—That would mess anybody's mind up, she says.

—I'm still not sure why, but their bio dad wanted them back at that point—and got them. I had never adopted them or anything, so I didn't have any legal … But I was so fucked up … I didn't even put up much of a fight.

—What could you've done?

I shrug.

—No way a court would award me custody when their biological father wanted them, but … I didn't … I didn't fight for them. That's the thing. I should've at least tried to keep them. Then … they'd know … I tried to stay in touch, to visit, but he made it nearly impossible. Then he moved them away, and … But I should've done more. I should've tried harder.

—Not much you could've done, she says. And with what you had been through …

—Could've done more. *Should* have. I just felt so guilty. So responsible.

—For?

—Huh?

—What do you feel guilty about, responsible for?

—Everything.

She nods, and it'd be so easy to leave it at that, not to tell her what I've never told anyone, and to continue carrying around what I have for so long. But something inside me wants to confess.

I start to say something, but stop, unable to give words to the cancer inside me.

—What? she asks. What is it?

—Nothing.

—Tell me.

—I … I was just so miserable I couldn't breathe, I say.

She nods.

—I wanted out, but the kids and I were so happy together—even given the challenges with Kevin, but … Monica and I were just … we … I … I couldn't leave her and I knew she wouldn't leave me … Neither of us could do that to the kids and so …

—And so … What'd you do?

—There were times … I actually … wished … her … wished she. Sometimes I wanted her to die.

—And she did, Regan says. And you felt responsible.

—I never thought I caused it or anything, but … yeah. I felt—still feel … so fuckin' guilty.

Regan slides over toward me in the seat and pulls me to her, holding me close to her.

—A whole lot of us wish certain people would die, she says. Yours just happened to. Doesn't make you responsible, doesn't mean you should feel guilty.

—But—

—Think if all the things we wished came true, she says. If even just a fraction of them. Wishing doesn't do anything. You didn't do anything.

—I did. I'm not saying I caused it, but to even want it—or think I did …

She nods, her thick hair rubbing my cheek as she does.

And then I begin to cry.

—Let it out, she says. Let it all out.

I do.

Dreams.

Monica is alive. We're in a waiting room of some kind—maybe a hospital. No. A funeral home.

I'm confused. I look around, searching for some clue as to where I am and why I'm here.

—You don't love me, she says.

—I do, I whisper, looking around at the other people in the small room.

—Not the way I love you.

—I love you. I do.

—But you're not *in* love with me.

—That seems a pretty juvenile distinction to me, I say.

I find the conversation embarrassing, and look around to see who's listening to us.

—I always did embarrass you.

—No, you didn't. You don't.

—Liar.

Suddenly, I'm in a viewing room of a funeral home, Casey's standing beside me in front of Monica's coffin.

There's something off about Casey—her age and … what? I'm
not sure. She appears to be at an age between late teens and the twenty-
something she is now—an age I never saw. And she's not exactly herself.
She looks similar, but there are slight differences.

—Why'd you kill her? she asks.

—I didn't.

—But you wanted her dead.

—No. No. Of course not. It was just a fleeting thought. I didn't
mean … didn't really want it to—

—And now you let me die. Why?

—No. I didn't. I mean … I'm so … sorry. Please forgive me.
Please don't—

We are alone in the room and there are no flowers.

—Why aren't there any flowers? I ask.

—No one loved her.

—That's not true. Everyone—

—You didn't.

—I did. I did. You know I did.

Now Casey's in the coffin and Monica is standing beside me again.

—How could you, Merrick?

—What?

—It's one thing to kill me, but my daughter? Why? Why would
you do that? Do you hate me so much that you would—

—No. I didn't. I didn't mean to let her—I tried to find her.

From within the coffin, Casey opens her eyes.

—It's okay, Daddy, she says. It's okay. I'm just sleeping. Wake me up. Wake me up. Dad, wake up. Wake up, Dad.

I wake in a cool, clean room on a comfortable bed.

I can tell it's a hotel room, but have no idea which one or how I got here.

Regan is talking softly on her cell phone in the bathroom, her hushed tones echoing out of the small, tile enclosure, but I can't make out anything she's saying.

I'm trying to get out of bed when she walks into the room wearing a white hotel bathrobe. Her dark hair is wet and hangs down over the robe in long, rope-like loops.

—Good morning, I say.

—Good afternoon, she says.

—Tell me I didn't miss … I say, gesturing between us.

—We slept together in only the most literal way. When we do it in the other way you won't be able to forget it.

I smile, but it quickly fades when I think about Casey.

—I don't remember anything after my little breakdown in the car.

—Little? she asks with a smile.

—It wasn't?

—There's a reason you don't remember.

—Sorry.

—Don't be. I'm so glad I was there.

—Where are we?

—Closest hotel I could find, she says. Not many left out here. It's all condos and townhouses.

—You stayed all night?

—Of course.

—How much was the room?

—Less than I make—made—in two hours.

—I'm so sorry to have put you through all this. It's embarrassing.

—Shouldn't be. It was no big deal at all. I told you. I love you. I was happy to be able to do something for *you* for a change.

I glance under the covers to see that I only have on underwear.

—You undressed me?

She nods.

—Wasn't easy with my eyes closed, she says.

—And you didn't take advantage of me?

—I was a perfect gentleman, she says.

—What've you got on under that robe?

She looks down at it, rubbing down the front and pulling on the belt.

—Less than you have on under those covers.

—So … nothing?

—Yeah, but … I realize we're half naked, alone in a hotel room, but …

—Yeah?

—There's certain lines we haven't crossed. Mind if we wait until I'm able to talk to Gabe?

—Can't imagine I'm very appealing after last night, I say.

—I'm more attracted to you now than I've ever been to anyone.

—How long was I out?

—Close to ten hours.

—I better get in the shower. Got a lot to do.

—Like what?

—Most pressing? Find Kevin and kill the fuck out of whoever killed Casey.

I stand in the shower, the scalding hot water searing my skin red raw, trying to feel it. For a long moment, I am unable to move, and so just stand here burning.

As my grogginess fades and I emerge more fully from the underworld of dreams and nightmares, I'm aware of more, remember more, yet don't feel any more.

It's as if I'm deep, deep down inside my own body—detached, distant, divorced from whatever connects me to me and the world.

I feel like I've just survived an enormous explosion and I'm stumbling around the devastation, destruction, and dead bodies, feet unsteady, ears ringing, everything around me seeming a great distance away.

Nothing. That's what I feel. And I'm glad. All my pain and anger and guilt have been blown away—at least for the moment, and it's good. I can hunt down Casey's killer without distractions.

Later, I will mourn. Now, I'm relieved I am unable to.

—I'm so sorry, man, Rashard is saying.

We are on the back deck at Uncle Ernie's, the descending sun slanting in over the bay.

He is eating. I am still unable to.

—Know anything more? I ask.

He shakes his head.

Before meeting him, I had taken Regan to her car so she could drive over to the FSU campus for the Bay County Autism Support Group.

With the center closed for the weekend, it's our best and only hope of finding Kevin or who's keeping him.

—Don't go in for another hour, he says. I'll find out what I can and let you know, but it's early days.

—I thought the first few hours were the most critical to catching the killer.

He shrugs.

—Probably right, he says. I'm just a beat cop.

—How soon can I see her?

—Not up to me, but I'll ask and let you know.

—Was … was she … raped?

—Got nothin' to do with the investigation. Don't know any details.

—Would you tell me if you did?

He nods.

—I wouldn't want to, but I would. You'd bug me to—until I did. I'll find out everything I can and call you later. You might want to see what Sheriff Parker can find out or talk to Frank directly. Or what about some of your old sources?

—They dry up fast, I say. But I may have a cop here and there that still owe me a favor.

We are quiet a moment, and I look away.

The boats on the bay bob up and down, a child's toys in a small pond, the brisk breeze snapping flags, puffing sails, and causing rigging to clang. Beyond the bay, the buildings of Panama City Beach are black, burnished by the sinking sun behind them.

The entire scene is breathtakingly beautiful and peaceful, and I have to blink back tears and force myself to think about something else when I realize Casey will never again get to enjoy something as simple and common as this.

—I need to tell you something, he says.

I turn back toward him, my eyes taking a moment to adjust.

—I've known you a long time, he says. So I know what I'm talking about.

I wait, my heart quickening.

—You've been carrying this weight around for a while.

—Yeah?

—Since what happened to—since the accident.

I nod.

—And it's understandable—at least for a while, but it's been far too long. It really is. I mean, I ain't ever said anything 'cause I ain't been through it, but …

He looks at me, but I can't meet his eye.

—It's like you've been punishing yourself. Like you really don't want to be happy.

—I've tried. I just …

—Have you? By messin' around with a married stripper?

I don't say anything, just think about what he's said. Have I been punishing myself? For what surviving? For wondering what it'd be like if Monica died? At not fighting for Casey and Kevin? Is that what my thing with Regan is about? Something to keep me frustrated? Strung out? Second guessing?

—It's been bad for a long time, he says, and … I just wonder …

—What?

—With what's happened now … Are you gonna … Is it gonna get worse? You gonna come up with even more self-destructive shit to do?

We are quiet a long moment, his words and the concern behind him penetrating the shock-hardened soil of my psyche.

After a long while, I nod to myself and look back at him.

—After this is over, I'll see someone.

He nods.

We fall silent again, and this time I feel awkward and self-conscious.

—I heard you, I say. And I *will* do something about it, but right now all I can do is try to help find out what happened to Casey and who did it.

He nods again.

—Have they talked to the guy who reported her missing again?

He looks confused.

—You? he asks.

—No, the first time, I say. Ian King.

He shrugs again.

—I'm sure someone has or will soon. Like you said, the first hours are the most important. I just don't know.

—I need his address, I say.

He shakes his head.

—I'll get it one way or another. I just want to talk to him. Not gonna do anything stupid. I've followed a lot of cases over the years.

—Following is very different than leading.

—I realize that. I'm not trying to lead. Just saying I know how to stay out of the way—and I know how these things work.

He shakes his head.

—Come on, man, I say.

—I'm just looking out for you—for your own good. I understand how you feel, but trust me. You need to let the investigators handle this. They know what they're doing. You get involved, you could fuck up the case and help get him off—not to mention getting yourself hurt or killed.

I nod.

—I'm gonna try not to get in the way, I say, but I *am* gonna do this. I have to.

Rashard's probably right. Odds are the case will flow more smoothly if I'm not running about mucking things up, but as a reporter I followed too many cases where the detectives involved had way too many cases to do them all justice. Those assigned to Casey's murder will be working other cases, too. I'm focused exclusively on hers. The cops on her case will want to still have personal lives—to go home, to rest and relax, to enjoy their weekends. I won't do anything, but this. I can't. And no matter how good the cops involved are, no matter how much they care, this is just another case to them. It has to be. For me, right now, this is everything.

Driving toward Ian King's place on the beach, I tap in his number.

—Hello, a voice thick with sleep or booze or both says.

—Ian?

—Yeah?

—I'm calling about Amber.

As far as Rashard could determine, Ian has not been notified about Casey's death—and won't be because he's not related to her and has not been ruled out as a suspect. Since he reported her missing under the name of Amber, I decide to use it.

—You a client? he asks.

—A what? I ask, then try to recover. Oh, yeah. A client. Yeah, I am.

—Who is this? he says.

—Just a client.

—Whatcha want?

—I need to talk to Casey.

—Who?

—I mean Amber, I say. Isn't Casey her real name?

—She uses a lot of names. The fuck's this about?

—I told you. You haven't heard from her?

—No, man, he says. She's missing.

—When's the last time you saw her?

—Monday. Why?

—*Monday?*

I had seen her on Wednesday and Thursday nights. Obviously, she hadn't been missing since Monday. Had she moved out? Was she trying to leave him? What about Kevin?

—Yeah, he says. Why?

—Where was she going?

—She had a gig.

—A gig?

—A client.

—Where? Where does she work?

—What?

—What kind of job? I say.

—You know. The thing she does.

—Does she live with you?

—Yeah, he says. She did. What's with all the fuckin'—

—How about Kevin? Is he there?

—What? The fuck is Kevin?

—Are you at home? Where do you live?

He ends the call, but I don't mind. I'll be pulling into his driveway inside of five minutes.

Anxiety.

Depression.

Regret.

Rashard is right. I have been living under such an enormous weight of remorse, feeling so responsible, so guilty. How could I not have seen it? Have I been punishing myself? Is my relationship with Regan a part of that? I don't want to think so, but I've got to. I have to consider that I'm involved with an often unreachable, ultimately unavailable woman to keep from—what? Truly connecting.

How many other self-destructive things am I doing?

Could I still have my job if I had fought for it?

How many friends and lovers and opportunities have I missed because I wouldn't let myself pursue anything that might actually be genuine, rewarding, fulfilling?

I can't believe I haven't seen this before. Now that I have … I've got to … What? What do I do? Awareness is a start, is something, but I have no idea what to do next. I guess I should talk to someone, but who? I think about it. I could go to a counselor, of course, and I will, but I'd like to start with someone I know. And then it hits me. Liz Jameson. After this is over, I'll find Liz and talk to her. She'll probably be able to recommend a good counselor, too.

Ian King lives in a modest home between Front Beach and Thomas Drive not far from the bridge. There are several like it left on the beach—the homes of individuals who didn't sell to developers during the bubble, who like living on the beach in spite of the cheap, gaudy tourist trap, in addition to other things, it is.

A pimped out older model Cadillac sits in the driveway, a small truck at an angle on the far edge of the yard, having pulled in straight off the street.

Ian, a young man in his mid-twenties, comes to the door in loose, light blue jogging pants, wife beater, matching blue cap, and an excessive amount of gold and platinum jewelry.

—I'm here about the missing persons report you filed, I say, pushing in past him, got a few questions for you.

He closes the door behind us.

The large room is overly full of furniture and cluttered—computers, exercise equipment, video game systems, and boxes and boxes of clothes, CDs, and DVDs.

—Just move in? I ask.

—No.

—Oh.

I turn around to face him. He doesn't offer me a seat, so we stand—me against the back of the couch, him with a hand propped on a dining table chair.

—You reported Casey missing on—

—The fuck is Casey? Amber. I reported Amber missing. You the fool just called?

—I was told you called and reported Casey missing, but that you called her Amber.

—Don't know nothin' 'bout no Casey.

—I thought you said she uses different names.

—Her real name is Amber. She's my girlfriend. She's been missing almost a week now.

He seems as confused as I am, and I try to figure out what's going on. Why did John Milton tell me he reported Casey missing if he didn't?

I think back to my initial conversation with the sheriff, trying to recall if he ever used a name—Casey or Amber. He didn't. He just said something like did you call about Miss Thunder Beach last night—but Casey *is* Miss Thunder Beach, so what does Amber have to do with any of this? Is it possible the answer is nothing? Are there two different missing person's cases that have gotten intertwined? But how? How could that—

—You a cop? he asks.

I nod.

—Working with them, I lie. Tell me about Amber.

His description of her matches Casey exactly.

—She a dancer? Part of the Miss Thunder Beach competition?

He shakes his head.

—Not this year. Has in the past. She does massage therapy. Involved in it that way this time.

I know from various stories I had worked on over the years that massage therapy is often a front for prostitution.

—You got a picture of her?

—She's on the front of the Thunder Beach Magazine, he says, beginning to look around the stacks in the room.

So he's talking about Casey. Casey is on the front of the magazine. Why does he think her name is Amber?

—Here it is.

He withdraws a copy of the magazine from a stack of them and hands it to me.

The publication is the same as the one with Casey, but from an earlier event, and the girl on the front, though she could pass as Casey's sister, maybe even twin, is not, in fact, Casey.

—This is Amber?

—Yeah.

—It says she's Miss Thunder Beach.

—Was, he says. Last spring.

I look at the dates of the magazine. It's the one from the rally this past autumn.

They publish the winner of the spring rally in the autumn edition and the winner of the autumn rally in the spring edition.

I recall now that there are two rallies, but because the one in the fall is so much smaller than the one in the spring, I think of Thunder Beach being every spring, though it's actually both.

So, Casey won the competition at the autumn rally and Amber won it last spring, but why would they think I was calling about Amber when I first called the publication's office? True, I hadn't used her name, just said I was calling about the girl on the cover, but even so, they should've assumed I meant the most recent—and then I remember.

What was it the guys at the booth outside Mrs. Newby's had said? They had to pass out the old edition while waiting to get some of the new ones in. I thought they were talking about different printings of the same edition, but they meant an earlier publication.

My mind begins to race.

Both blondes, both Miss Thunder Beach, both missing. Can't be a coincidence. But which one's dead? Is it possible Casey's still alive?

My pulse quickens and I feel hope begin to fill me, emanating outward from a tiny wishful spark in the center of me.

—What have the police told you? I ask.

—Nothin'. Won't tell me shit.

—Did Amber having anything to do with this year's Thunder Beach?

He shakes his head.

—Not officially. She crowned the new one last fall, and that's it. She did have some clients coming in for it.

—Clients?

—I told you, man. She's a massage therapist.

—And she had clients coming in for Thunder Beach?

—Yeah. It's her busiest week of the year. Where are you going?

Running to my car, I call Rashard.

He doesn't answer.

As I drive away, I leave a detailed message explaining everything I've just learned.

I then call John Milton and do the same thing, asking him to notify all law enforcement in the area.

I cut my message a little short when Tristan beeps in.

—Any luck on identifying the cat in the picture yet? he asks.

—Not so far.

—Looks so familiar. I know I've seen him somewhere. Gonna pass it around today. Should have something for you soon. It's like it's on the tip of my brain—just need something to jog my memory.

He doesn't know anything about the cops believing Casey to be dead, so I don't mention Ian or anything he said.

—You able to get Brad and the boys out?

—Heading there now. They wouldn't let me last night.

—Thank them again for me. Tell 'em I owe 'em.

—Will do. Ciao.

I call Regan next.

It takes her a while to answer, and when she does, she talks very softly.

—Casey might still be alive, I say.

—What? Hold on, let me step outside. How? Are you sure?

I tell her what Ian told me.

—Oh my God, Merrick. That's just the best news. The best. Should I stop trying to find Kevin?

—No. Keep trying. How's it going?

—I think I'm getting pretty close. These are the nicest people. I'll call you when I have something. Better get back in. I'm so happy for you. Let me know what you find out.

When we end the call, I become aware of where I am—15th Street between the Port and the college, surrounded by motorcycles. As I take a left on 23rd, I search for Bay County Medical Examiner on my phone, and find that it's on Frankford over near the airport.

I'm nearing Frankford when Rashard calls back.

—How the fuck this happen? he says.

—They fit the same description, both won Miss Thunder Beach, were on the cover—of different issues, but they were both being passed out this weekend. When I called and asked about the girl on the cover and described her, the woman taking the call assumed I meant the girl she had already been called about—Amber. Ian had already reported her missing by then.

—So she who's in the morgue?

—I'll know if I can see her, I say. I'm headed there now. Can you get me in?

—They haven't even done the autopsy yet.

—I'm almost there. Make some calls. Let Frank know what's going on. You've got to get me in. I've got to know—hell, the detectives heading up the investigation have to know.

—I'll see what I can do, but I can tell you it ain't gonna happen.

—Thanks.

When I walk out of the ME's office, Rashard is waiting on me, in uniform, leaning against his patrol car.

He pushes himself up.

—Couldn't wait any longer, I say. Went in to see if I could talk them into letting me view the body.

—And?

I shake my head.

—Told you.

—I don't get it. We've got to know. How can they investigate if they don't know who they're victim is?

—I've got a way we can do it, he says.

—How?

—Crime scene photos.

I nod.

—Great idea, I say. Where are they?

—I've got 'em with me, but just hold on a minute. You've got to prepare yourself. It could still be Casey. And if it's not, they're still unpleasant as hell to look at.

—I understand. I'm ready.

—You sure?

—Yeah. Come on.

He reaches is into the open window of his car and withdraws a file folder. Opening it, he begins to flip through the pictures.

—Let me find the best one for identification, he says.

I snatch the folder from him and begin to examine the pictures.

The small, pale body is splayed out atop the bunched up and wadded white sheets of a hotel bed. Though there's no blood or any obvious signs of violence, her smeared lipstick and tear- and mascara-streaked cheeks do tell a story with an unhappy ending—and it's clear the girl is dead, not sleeping.

It's not Casey, and this makes me so happy that I feel like a monster. How can I look at this poor, abused, and abandoned girl and be glad she is dead? And that's what it is. I am glad it's her and not Casey. A wave of nausea rises up from the pit of my stomach, and I think I'm going to vomit.

—Well? Rashard asks.

I shake my head.

—It's not Casey, I say.

—You sure?

I nod.

—How?

—She has a scar on her leg from her twelfth birthday party at Miracle Strip.

—You okay?

—Yeah. Will be.

—You think that's Amber? he asks, nodding toward the folder I've now closed.

—Don't know who else it could be.

—Any idea what the fuck's goin' on?

—None. But I'm not thinking it's a coincidence they both were part of the Thunder Beach pageant. They were actually on stage together this past fall.

—Think the killer saw them then? If so, why wait 'til now? That's a long time.

—Could just come here for Thunder Beach, I say. You could do a search for similar victims around the country. Might let us know where he's from—help figure out who it is.

—Great idea, he says. I'll pass it along.

—So we're thinking the same guy that killed Amber has Casey?

—Too many similarities not to consider, he says, turning toward his car. I've got to let the lead detective know all this. I'm sure he'll want to talk to you.

Back in my car, I'm so happy, so relieved, I can hardly drive.

The euphoria I'm experiencing is far better than the best drug I've ever taken.

As if on a loop, my mind keeps repeating: She's still alive. She's still alive. She's still alive.

She is, another voice in my head says, but she won't be for long. Don't celebrate until you have her safely back, unharmed.

My mind continues its loop, but with a different mantra now: She's still out there. She's still out there. She's still out there.

I've got to find her—and fast—or the next victim in a crime scene photo I see will be her.

—**Y**ou're pretty good at this, Frank Clemmons says. Ever thought about being a detective?

I laugh.

Frank Clemmons, a detective with the Panama City Police Department, is the lead investigator in Amber's death. He's a thick, but fit, gray-haired man in his late fifties with tanned, puffy skin.

I've just finished telling him everything I know about Amber and Casey and what I've been up to the past few days—sans the break-in at The Dollhouse.

—I'm serious, he says. We got three agencies working this thing and you've found out more than all of us put together.

—Not very different from chasing down a story, I say, but, truth is, this is personal. I'm highly motivated.

He nods.

We're seated in the front booth of Pizzeria Napoli at the corner of 22 and Business 98 in Springfield.

We're here because he was in the area conducting an interview, but it's by far my favorite pizza, and with my appetite back, there's nowhere I'd rather be.

Since Amber's body was found in a room at the Marie Motel in downtown, Panama City PD is handling the case, but because she lived on the beach and because of the possible connections to the rally, several agencies are involved—including the Bay County Sheriff's Department and Panama City Beach PD.

I take another bite of my pizza and savor the taste on my tongue. Though every aspect of the pie at Pizzeria Napoli is delicious, it's the hand-tossed, homemade garlic butter crust that separates it from every other pizza I've tried.

—So, he says, the guy who threatened you when you were leaving Newby's and the calls you got Wednesday night, think those were about Amber or Casey?

I shrug.

—I think Amber, but no way to know, is there?

—Not 'til we find the fucker and ask him.

I think back to the calls from Wednesday night. No one ever used a name—just Miss Thunder Beach. I try to recall the magazine the man in the parking lot held up when warning me off. At the time, I thought it was an alternative cover of Casey or an earlier edition, but now I believe it was an older issue with Amber's picture on it.

Even Regan's response to the cover was strange. I had both issues that night. Which one did I show her? It must have been the one of Amber—the one I first found inside Mrs. Newby's. What was it she said later in the club when I asked her about it? I don't think I know her, but I think I know who you mean. Something like that.

As usual, the TV mounted in the back left corner of Pizzeria Napoli shows The Food Network. A gray-haired southern woman is talking while stirring items into a skillet, though I can neither hear her nor make out the items.

—How long you been a detective? I ask.

—Coming up on twenty-six years.

—So you've seen a lot, I say.

He nods.

—Too much, he says.

—You got a read on whether Amber's overdose was accidental or—

—Whether it was or not, she wasn't alone.

—How do you—

—It didn't happen at the Marie. Somebody dumped the body there.

I nod and think about it.

—Was there anything—a signature or something—that makes you think you're dealing with a serial—

—Nothing yet. Too soon to tell.

—Had she been raped?

—She'd had vigorous intercourse—not sure if it was consensual or not.

I nod, and wonder why he's being so forthcoming. I don't have to wonder long.

—Remember the Alfonzo Williams case? he asks.

I nod again.

I had reported on it, had actually written a series of articles about it. A white cop had shot and paralyzed a black kid, in what was believed to be a racially motivated shooting.

—The cop involved, he says. Colvin.

—Yeah?

—He's a good friend of mine—like a son to me. He's a good man. It was a righteous shoot.

I nod.

—You were the first and only one to say so for a long time, he adds.

—Just wrote the facts.

—Saved his career. Maybe his life.

I shoot him an incredulous look.

—Cops don't last long inside, he says. I owe you for that, and for what you've turned up in this case, so I'm gonna give you some advice.

Here we go, I think. Back off and let the cops deal with this.

—We're good at what we do, he says. But we move slow. Can't be helped. The way the system's set up. I know of victims who were alive when we figured out where they were likely to be and dead by the time we got a warrant.

I nod again, wondering if he's telling me what I think he is.

—I'm not saying do anything stupid or rash. You do, you'll get yourself and the girl killed, but this was my daughter or stepdaughter or niece or someone I cared about, I wouldn't wait on us, I'd go off the reservation if I had to.

—Thanks.

—I'm not saying try to catch this prick. I'm saying keep doing what you're doing. Keep digging. You find something, you let us know. You let *me* know, and I'll take this cocksucker down.

—I will.

—Like I said, you're good at this. The clock is ticking. We got one dead girl. Don't want another.

While I was meeting with Clemmons, I missed a call from Tristan, but before calling him back, I tap in Regan's number.

Getting her voicemail, I ask her to call me as soon as she can, tell her I love her, end the call, then call Tristan.

—You get my message? he asks.

—Didn't take time to listen to it, I say. Figured it'd be quicker just to call you back.

—Cool. Well, get this.

—Yeah?

—Brad recognizes the guy in the picture. Said he'd know that awful fuckin' haircut anywhere.

—What? Who is it?

—Doesn't know his name, but knows where he works.

—Where?

—Jade Gardens, he says.

—What is—

—The massage parlor on Front Beach.

—Let me call you right back, I say.

—Okay.

When he's gone, I call Ian King.

—Where does Amber work? I ask.

—Who is—

—You said she did massage therapy, I say. Where?

—She did a lot of outcall work.

I knew from a story I had done about sex trafficking that outcall was a term used mostly by escort services for in-home visits. Outcall, the escort goes to the client. Incall, the client goes to the escort. Like a lot of massage parlor workers, I'm betting Amber was a prostitute.

—But when it's incall, I say. Where is it?

—Jade Gardens. Why?

—Thanks.

I end the call and bring up Tristan again.

—Can you have Brad meet me at Jade Gardens? I ask.

—Why?

—Because, I say, I'm about to go off the reservation.

Jade Gardens Oriental Massage Parlor is a storefront joint in a strip mall not far from the Y on Panama City Beach.

Like so many fronts for prostitution or even sex work, Jade Gardens has a locked wrought iron door that must be buzzed open.

When I ring the bell, a small, middle-aged Asian woman with short, black hair opens the interior door and looks me over through the iron bars.

—You want massage?

I nod.

—Seventy dollar.

I pull out four twenties and hand them to her through the bars.

She buzzes me in and doesn't offer change.

The reception area is small, with soiled furniture that doesn't match, and a funky smell I can't identify.

I stop and look around, trying to take it all in.

There's a counter with a small TV on it and an opening with a beaded curtain hanging down.

—You go this way, she says, pointing to the left down a narrow hallway with doors on each side.

I turn and hit the button to buzz open the door, and Brad enters.

—You no do that, she shouts. I call cops.

—Go ahead, I say, pulling out the picture of Little Caesar and holding it up. I'm sure they'd like to talk to this guy, too.

—No. You leave now. Want no trouble.

—Where is he?

—He no here. No work here no more.

—You fire him 'cause he killed Amber?

—We not kill no one. You leave. NOW.

—I no leave without him, I say.

Brad laughs.

—What kind a joint you running here? I ask. Just happy endings or hardcore?

—I no tell you nothing Mr. Motherfucker.

—We're gonna have a look around, Brad says. You sit down and shut up.

—This my place. You no tell me shut up in my place. Hey I recognize you. You been here before Mr. Bad Bone.

I laugh.

—Bitch, that's Mr. Big Bone. Just ask your girls.

—They say you Mr. Limp Dick Motherfucker.

—Yeah, I say, I heard that, too.

I head down the hallway. Starting at the end, I open each door. Three are empty, five have bare breasted women giving hand jobs, one has full-on fucking.

Based on the nationality of the workers and the fact that they appear to be living here, I'm pretty sure many of these girls are the victims of trafficking.

—Health inspection, I yell. How many licensed massage therapists we got here?

The workers yell—joining the rants coming from the lady up front—johns scatter, clutching their clothes as they rush out.

When I open the final door, the man from the photo steps forward and presses a small revolver to my forehead.

—You want see him now, Mr. Limp Dick? the small Asian woman, who has just run up behind me, asks.

—I'm Mr. Motherfucker, I say. Brad's Mr. Limp Dick.

—You all look alike, cracker ass cracker motherfucker.

I back down the hallway and into the reception area, hands raised.

—Fuck you now, the small woman says. Get fuck outta my place.

—Don't worry, Jade, the man says. Takin' out the trash is part of my job.

—That include Amber? I ask.

—Don't forget other one, Jade says.

The man looks confused, but before he can ask what she means, Brad steps through the beaded curtain and places a gun of his own into the back of the man's head.

—Drop it, Brad says.

I hear something in Brad's voice I've never heard before.

—Bet I can shoot him before you can—

Brad hits the man so hard with the butt of his gun it sounds like his skull cracks open. He falls to the ground, unconscious, bangs the front part of his head on the floor and drops his gun.

—Bet you can't, Brad says. I win.

I pick up the gun and look at Brad admiringly.

—Thanks.

—Haven't done anything yet. Thank me when we get the girl back.

I'm more disturbed by what I saw in Jade Gardens than anything in recent memory—mostly because of my own culpability in its existence.

Exploitation always angers me.

And there seems to be more of it now than ever before. We're living in a fucking domination system where the powerful do whatever the fuck they want with impunity, a world of nation-corporations where the rich eat the poor and congratulate themselves on winning, as if what they're destroying are the plastic toy figures of a board game instead of the lives of actual human beings.

Predatory politicians, preachers, and pundits prey on the weak and vulnerable, their self-centered existences devoid of empathy, mercy, doubt, and remorse.

But nothing incenses me like the sexual abuse of women—whether domestic violence, rape, or sexual slavery, I'm never filled with homicidal rage as much as when confronted with this form of pitilessness and brutality.

And this form of exploitation is on the rise.

Sexual Trafficking, the recruitment, transportation, transfer, harboring, or receipt of persons for the purposes of commercial sexual exploitation, is estimated to involve somewhere between seven hundred thousand and four million women, children and men each year.

Of course, when most people hear the word trafficking, they think of poor, lawless third-world countries, but yearly, right here in the land of the free, an estimated 14,500 to 17,500 women and children are trafficked. The United States has become a destination location for commercial sex exploitation and slavery. Sex trafficking has been reported in at least twenty different states, with most cases occurring in New York, California, and Florida. In fact, Florida is being inundated with trafficked women from Russia, the Ukraine, and Central Europe.

Traffickers typically lure women to the U.S. with false promises of jobs as waitresses, nannies, and models.

Women are prevented from leaving by security guards, violence, threats, debt bondage, and retention of documents. The traffickers maintain control through isolation—in many instances, the women must live and work at the same location.

Once imprisoned (and no matter what it looks like that's what it is), the women usually find themselves being threatened with physical abuse against themselves and their families in order to force cooperation. Traffickers also play upon the women's fears of arrest and deportation.

The girls are moved around a lot—from town to town in makeshift brothels—mobile homes, campers, rented houses, apartments, hotel rooms. If they're ever caught and arrested, their exploiters bail them out and move them to a different city.

But it's not just women and children from other countries who are being treated so inhumanely. Every day young girls are being abducted or coerced and forced into sexual surrogacy by boyfriends and others they think they can trust—raped and abused in unimaginable ways, the threat of death, for them or their families, hanging over them at all times.

I'm reminded of Liz Jameson, and the story I'm going to write for her. I've got to call her, to get her involved with this.

What makes me feel even worse is about a year ago I had been contacted by a reporter in South Florida working on a story about the international sex slave trade. The *Miami Herald* was doing a piece on the prevalence of sex trafficking in Florida, and she wanted to know if it extended into the Panhandle. I had learned a lot about sex trafficking at the time, but I had failed to find any victims and concluded that it hadn't made it to Panama City. Failed is right. I had an opportunity to expose something most Americans can't even fathom—that slavery never ended in this great country—and I blew it.

Jade Gardens is still in operation, still in the business of slavery and rape because I didn't do my damn job.

But am I culpable in other ways? Does my use of porn or my patronizing strip clubs in some small way enable, even encourage sex trafficking? It's difficult to think about, but I have to, have to examine my actions and their consequences—even the unintended ones.

On the drive over to the address Brad gave me, I try Regan again.

Still no answer.

After leaving her another message, I call Liz Jameson, tell her what I found at Jade Garden, and recruit her to assist the victims there and to help find Casey.

When we finish, I call Frank Clemmons.

—Place on Front Beach, I say. Jade Garden.

—Yeah?

—Massage parlor. Pretty sure it has a connection to Amber's murder and Casey's disappearance. Amber worked there and so does the guy Casey left the club with.

—Motherfucker.

—What?

—We sent a deputy over there earlier in the week when we found out Amber worked there.

—And?

—And, had he done his damn job, we'd've known about this sooner.

—Even if there's no connection, I say, I'm pretty sure there are sex slaves working and living there.

—Shit like that brings out the worst in me.

—I can't think of anyone better to unleash it on.

Brad had told me to give him half an hour or so before meeting him. After talking to Rashard and trying Regan again, it takes me about forty-five minutes.

The address he gave me is an abandoned house trailer on the east end of the beach. It's one of two remaining in what was a mobile home community and was to become a townhouse subdivision before the housing bust.

The day over, the night not quite here, the limbo-like moment one of gloom, as if trapped between the sun and the moon.

The dim, dusky evening atmosphere adds to the menacing mood draped like a shroud over the mobile home.

I knock on the door, but there's no answer. Pushing it open, I step into the dark, damp dwelling.

I pause a moment for my eyes to adjust.

All the windows are blacked out, most of the furniture has been removed, and the carpet is soggy from rain water that has poured in from a leaking roof.

I follow the only light and sound down a narrow hallway to the very back room.

In it, I find the man from the massage parlor bound to a chair, beaten and bloodied, whimpering beneath the duct tape covering his mouth.

The four high-powered flashlights trained on him illuminate a series of cuts and slashes I assume are the result of the large knife Brad is holding.

—Right on time, Brad says, as I walk in.

—For what?

—To hear this canary sing.

I look at him quizzically.

—Watched a film noir marathon last weekend, he explains.

I think about all the ways I've condemned torture in articles and columns I've written over the years and what a hypocrite I am.

—Aren't you? Brad asks the man.

He nods vigorously and attempts to say something from beneath the tape.

—Ask him anything you like, Brad says.

—Where's Casey?

Brad rips the tape off his mouth.

More tears flow out of his eyes and down the swollen skin of his pain-filled face.

—Who?

Brad steps forward and slices the skin between the first two fingers of the guy's left hand, which looks to be taped down especially for this purpose.

He screams.

When I look at his right hand, I can see that Brad has already used up the four spaces there.

—Tell me who that is. I'll tell you the truth. I swear to God. Just tell me. I don't know a Casey.

—Tiffany, I say. From The Dollhouse. You left with her.

—Oh. Her. Yeah. No. I don't know where she is now.

Brad moves toward him.

—Wait. Wait. I'm not lying. I handed her off to this guy. I'll tell you everything. Just don't cut me.

—Need to cut your damn hair, Brad says.

—What guy? I ask.

—Don't know any of their names. I swear.

—This isn't helping, I say, and we don't have time to be fuckin' around. Start from the beginning.

—And you better tell the fuckin' truth, Brad adds.

—I will. I swear. I swear. These guys with money. They come down during Thunder Beach and want to party while they're here. Want girls. You know? Sometimes I help with girls. Escorts, strippers, whatever. They pay me a small finders fee for finding what they're looking for and supplying it. Some want a black girl or a fat girl or a young girl. This one guy wants Miss Thunder Beach, wants Amber Nicole. Willing to pay big money. She's up for it. It's what she does. You know? So we do the deal. I get my little fee. Life goes on. Next thing I know, she doesn't show up for work, won't answer her phone, disappears. A few days later, I get a call from this guy saying there's a problem. He needs another girl—one that looks like the first one. I was like where the fuck am I gonna get a girl that looks like the other one. But I have to, you know, 'cause now he's offering an insane amount of money. Guy he works for really, really wants a girl that looks like Amber Nicole. Anyway, so I'm tellin' this to a buddy of mine, and he says, the judges of the Miss Thunder Beach competition must have the same taste as this guy 'cause the girl they picked in the fall looks just like the one they picked last spring—Amber. Said he knew her, her name, where she worked, everything.

—What's your buddy's name?

—He's more of a real good customer. Comes in to see Amber all the time. Think she reminds him of this other chick.

—His name, I say.

—Vic.

—Dyson?

His eyes widen a bit.

—Yeah, he says. You know him?

—So what happened next?

—He tells me she works nights over at The Dollhouse, so I take a couple of grand and I go see her. Come up with this story—my son's in the hospital, it's his birthday, he's turning twenty-one today. All he wants is a lap dance by a beautiful woman. All I want is to make him happy. I'll give her two grand just to come to Bay Medical and give him two dances.

—She fell for that?

—Thing is, I know this guy who's in the hospital. I pay him to tell her this story if she calls. So when she wants verification, I give her his name. She calls the hospital, asks for him, is told his room number, and is transferred up to it. They talk. She says okay. She could really use the money. I give her a thousand up front, show her the other, then we go. At the hospital, everything goes real well. My friend sells it well. I pay her. So now she's got two grand—and I tell her, you wanna make three more I've got a friend having a bachelor party out on the beach. Show her the other three G's, tell her it's a public place, she'll be safe, and …

—She goes?

—Yeah.

—Where?

—La Vela. The guy's waiting there for her. They meet. He approves. Pays me. I'm gone. Last I seen of her.

—We went to La Vela looking for her that night, I say. No one had seen her.

—They were in the Posh Ultralounge.

—It was closed.

—For everyone else. They had it by themselves 'til after the concert.

I shake my head. I was there, so close to her—and didn't even know it.

—You threw around a lot of money, Brad says. How much did he pay you for the girl?

—Twenty.

—Thousand?

—Yeah.

Brad looks at me.

—What?

—He bought her, he says.

—What?

—We don't find her, she's not coming back.

I look at the guy bound to the chair.

—So, I say, where can we find her?

—I swear to Christ I don't know.

—Where can we find the guy then?

—I just don't know. I swear. He's just a middleman, wouldn't do you any good anyway, but I don't know. I'm not lying. I've told you everything.

—How does he contact you?

—Phone.

—You got his number?

—Always blocks it.

Brad looks at me.

—You believe him? he asks.

I shrug.

—I swear it's the truth. I've told you everything. I swear it. You can torture me some more and I can make some shit up, but I've told you everything.

Are you really doing this again? I say on Regan's voicemail. Now? Right now? With all that's going on you're disappearing on me again?

I'm racing down Back Beach toward Pier Park to test an idea I had.

When I left the trailer, Brad was about to take one more go at the man to make sure he had really told us everything he knew. When he finishes, he's going to let me know so I can call Frank Clemmons to pick him up.

—Listen, I say, if you really can't answer your phone for some reason—if something's happened or … I'll feel horrible, and I'm sorry, but I think, given our history, you'll understand why I might make the assumption I am. If you're bailing again, fine, I'm not surprised, but think about your timing. Just do me a favor. Text me with what you found out about Kevin. Please. If nothing else, please do that.

Driving way too fast, I dart in and out of traffic, attempting to be cognizant of the many motorcyclists, hoping I won't get pulled over.

When I finish the message for Regan, I call Rashard.

—Got a line on Vic Dyson yet? I ask.

—Put him on the back burner with everything else going on. Why?

—He's involved.

—How? And how do you know?

—He's the one who pointed Casey out to her abductor.

—You sure?

—Positive, I say. Think you can move him up to the front burner?

—Yeah, but he's a slippery little bitch. Paranoid 'cause he's always up to somethin'.

—Thanks.

—How you find out he's involved?

—Long story, I say. I'll tell you when I can. Gotta go.

I tap off the call before he can say anything else.

The last light of the setting sun is just a pink streak beneath a splash of indigo on the western horizon.

Even on Back Beach, the traffic is heavy and slow, and it takes me longer than I'd like to make it to Pier Park.

Pulling in the first entrance, I head directly to the AT&T Store and run inside.

The store is crowded, people lined up waiting their turn, and though Adam is helping a customer at his desk, I motion for him.

Excuse me just a moment, he says to the plump, sunburned tourist in the too-tight summer dress.

—What's up?

—Got an emergency, I say. Need your help and I don't have a lot of time.

—Okay.

—There a workstation in the back?

—Yeah. Give me just a second.

I'm filled with relief and gratitude—again, and I think about how much help I've received over the past few days. At first it seems remarkable, but then I realize that it's not only that most people genuinely love the opportunity to help when someone's in need, but that I'd chosen those most likely to say yes.

A communications major at FSU, Adam had interned with me a

couple of semesters ago, and we'd become friends. Smart, witty, tech-savvy, he's saved my computer, and therefore, my ass on more than one occasion.

He walks back over to his desk, and bends over to address the pale, puffy, red-streaked tourist.

Nearly six-six, Adam is lanky like the long, wavy black hair on his head that sways about as he moves.

—So sorry, he says, but I've got an emergency. All the questions you have can be answered on our website or you can call if we can assist you further.

He hands her his card and moves toward the back door before she can respond.

I follow him.

—What's going on? he asks when we're in the back.

I tell him.

—Damn, he says when I'm finished with a quick recount of Casey's predicament. I mean damn. What can I do?

—I noticed she had an iPhone, I say. Is there some way we can trace her?

—Possibly, he says.

I realize what I'm asking you to do is illegal or—

—Something like this, he says, shaking his head, his dark hair whipping around, is worth losing a job over.

—I hope it doesn't come to that, I say. I can't believe I didn't think of this sooner, but shortly after I thought she was missing, I found out she really wasn't, then after I found out she really was, they told me she was dead, so I've just been … But I should've thought of it. Probably too late now. Phone's probably dead or no longer with her, but …

—Let's see what we can do, he says. Family Map is probably the best way, but if she's the only one on the account she probably won't have it.

—Family Map?

—Program that lets you track the location of people in your plan through your phone or computer.

—Can I buy a phone, add it to her plan, and get the Family Map?

—You could, I guess, theoretically, but it'd send a text to her phone with a configuration code. She'd have to send it back to you and you'd have to enter it in before you could track her.

I nod.

—She may have it for her brother, I say. She'd want to be able to keep up with him.

—Let's pull up her account and take a look.

—I've got her number, I say, but I don't think the account is under her name.

—Just need the number.

I give it to him and he types it in.

—Bingo, he says. She has it.

—What's the address on the account? I ask.

—A PO Box on the beach.

I nod.

—What name?

—Monica Walsh.

—Her mom's name. Does it show where she is?

He shakes his head.

—It's the other number on the account, he says. Must be the brother.

—How close will it get us to where he actually is?

—Within six meters.

—Wow. Where is he?

—**M**errick McKnight, Kevin shouts when he sees me.

He rushes up to me, smiling, but stops short of hugging or even touching.

—Hey Kevin, I say, patting him on the shoulder, hoping it's okay. He doesn't seem to mind.

—Hey, Merrick.

Much bigger than the last time I saw him, Kevin has a large, soft pale, body with close-cropped, sandy blond hair and fingernails that need cutting—something he must still hate.

—How are you, buddy? It's been a long time.

—I'm GREAT, he says. It *has* been a long time. You know what, Merrick?

—What?

—Guess what?

—What?

As he talks, repeating himself often and placing emphasis on certain words, he rocks back and forth or paces, and uses his hands a lot.

Appearing behind him in the doorway, a small elderly woman with short, white hair and polyester pants eyes me suspiciously.

—This is Merrick McKnight, Kevin says. My good old friend, Merrick McKnight.

—I recognize Merrick from the pictures. Is Casey okay? How'd you find us? she asks.

—It's a long story and I don't have a lot of time, I say. I'm trying to find Casey.

—You know what Merrick? You know what? Casey … Casey didn't come home last night. We haven't seen her.

—I know, I say. I'm working with the police to find her.

—The POLICE, Kevin says. COO-OOL.

—You can call PCBPD and ask for an officer named Rashard or PCPD and ask for a detective named Clemmons, I say to the woman.

She shakes her head.

—Casey and Kevin have told me a lot about you, she says. Come in.

—Come in Merrick McKnight, Kevin says, bouncing back into the small house.

—Guess what, Merrick McKnight, he says. Guess what?

—What?

—Did you know—did you know left handed people are generally smarter, more often smokers, and die earlier than right handed people?

—I didn't know that, I say. Where'd you learn that?

The home is modestly furnished, clean, and neat. Among the family photos on a tall sofa table behind the couch is an old picture of me with a much younger Casey and Kevin.

—Did you know—did you know—did you know some species of fish have voices?

—I didn't.

—Hey. Hey Merrick McKnight. Did you know—did you know ninety-seven percent of all US money has traces of cocaine on it?

—I didn't. Hey, Kevin. Can I see your phone?

—Our phone? the lady asks.

—Cell phone, I say. Don't Casey and Kevin both have AT&T phones?

—Oh. I hold onto Kevin's for him when we're at home. He'd spend all his time playing with it if we'd let him.

—Have you heard from Casey? Has she tried to contact you on it or in any other way?

She shakes her head, then steps over to a small bookshelf beside the TV.

While we're talking, Kevin moves around whimpering, waiting his turn to speak again, gyrating like a small child needing to go to the bathroom.

—Merrick. Merrick McKnight. Did you know—did you know the word *set* has more definitions than any other word in the English language?

—I didn't. No. That's very interesting.

The woman steps back over to me and hands me an iPhone just like Casey's.

—Thanks.

—Oh *COO-OOL*, Kevin shouts, his eyes growing wide and lighting up when he sees the phone. The Apple iPhone 3G S. Fastest iPhone ever. And now with video, and, and, and a compass. And a better battery and screen and camera and, and, and voice recording.

As I unlock it and begin tapping through menus and apps, Kevin continues to pace and shimmy and scratch his head and talk incessantly.

—I need to borrow this, I say. I'll take good care of it and bring it back.

Kevin continues to talk about the features, but the woman nods.

—Everything's going to be okay, I say. I'm gonna bring Casey home and help take care of you. Would you like that?

—Yes. *I would* like that.

—Okay. I love you, buddy. I'll be back soon.

I pat him on the back and turn and head toward the door.

—Merrick McKnight. Merrick. Hey Merrick McKnight.

—Yeah? I say, pausing at the door, my hand on the knob.

—Hey Merrick. Did you know that—did you know that it takes seventeen muscles to smile, but forty-three to frown?

—I didn't, I say, opening the door. I always learn so much when

I'm around you. I've missed that. Can't wait to start hanging out more. A lot more.

—*Yeah.* That would be *coo-ool.*

—I'll be back soon with Casey and you can teach me some more then.

Got an anonymous tip for you, I say.

I'm in my car, fighting the traffic, attempting to get to La Vela. On the seat beside me, Kevin's phone is running the Family Map app, but Casey's is still not showing up. It's not that I think Casey is still at La Vela, but it's the last place I know for sure she went to, and it's where her abductors were.

—Not exactly anonymous, Frank Clemmons says. I know who this is.

—It's not coming from me so much as through me, I say.

—Huh?

—I received an anonymous tip and now I'm passing it on to you.

—Oh.

When Brad had called to say the cops could come pick up Casey's kidnapper since he had nothing else to give us, he said he was sorry but he had to get back to The Curve to help with the crowd. I had thanked him for all he had done and told him I understood, but heading to La Vela I wish I still had him around watching my back.

—There's a guy in an abandoned trailer on Sunrise Court who confessed to helping Casey's abductors gain access to her. Man who called me said he was roughing him up a bit over a drug deal that went bad and he tells him about the kidnapping.

—Interesting.

—I thought so.

—I hope you know what you're doing, he says.

—Well, I don't, but I'm doing what I can.

—When I said you might need to go off the res, I didn't mean leave the country.

After inching along Thomas Drive for what seems like hours, I finally arrive at La Vela. With my phone in one pocket and Kevin's in the other, I push through the crowd in the parking lot.

Beyond the club, out over the Gulf, lightning from an approaching storm dances in the distance.

Between vendor tents, tractor trailers, campers, and what looks to be thousands of parked bikes, each leaning to the left, the throng thrashes about. There's no way to get anywhere fast, so I practice patience, but persistence as I press through toward the entrance.

Thundering up and down Thomas Drive, the roar of the motorcycles is deafening, drowning out all other noises.

Periodically, I pull Kevin's phone out of my pocket and check to see if Case's is showing up again, but so far nothing.

When I first enter, the Metallica cover band in the Concert Coliseum is so loud, I can't hear anything else, so I quickly move toward the Thunderdome.

Like the previous night, all the other rooms are closed, their doors locked, but I wonder if there are private parties taking place in any of them.

Inside the Thunderdome, I tell a bartender I need to speak to a manager, and look around while I wait.

There are even more people than the night before, and I realize how ridiculous it is for me to be here by myself.

Stepping away from the bar and over to the restroom where it's a little quieter, I call Rashard. Getting his voicemail, I leave him a message telling him where I am, what I'm doing, and ask him to send help. Probably won't find anything here, probably be a waste of their time, but better that than—

When I turn around to head back out to the bar, the thick, muscular black man who'd threatened me in the parking lot Wednesday night is standing there.

Before I can do anything, his enormous fist shoots out into my midsection, knocking the breath out of me, sending arcs of pain out in every direction.

I drop my phone and it clangs on the floor.

Shoving me through the door of the closest stall, he slams me against the wall, placing his forearm beneath my chin and closing the door behind him.

Mouth open, frantic for air, I still can't breathe.

—Was I right? he asks.

I can't speak, but I must have looked perplexed.

—I told you a subsequent visit from me wouldn't be as pleasant.

There was nothing pleasant about the first one, I think, but am unable to say anything.

As I'm still trying to breathe and squirm away, he pulls a small syringe out of his pocket, pulls the cap off with his teeth, jams it into my neck, and plunges the contents into my bloodstream.

My heart rate drops.

My breathing slows.

The room begins to spin.

When he moves his forearm from my neck, I collapse, and within moments of hitting the floor, I begin vomiting.

Snatching me up, he pulls me out of the stall and out of the restroom.

Dragging me through the crowd, he feigns concern and sympathy.

I have a hard time keeping my eyes open, and only see flashes of faces, smears of motion, as people continue to pour into the club and move to the music.

From the effects I'm feeling, I'd say he gave me a shot of GHB. While working on a story about its use as a club drug and as a weapon of sexual assault for what is inaccurately known as date rape, I had learned a lot about it.

—What's wrong? someone asks.

My aching head pounds with the booming music, and I feel another wave of nausea begin.

—His ass is fucked up, the big guy carrying me says. That's what. Can't believe he pulled this shit the night I'm the DD.

—Should we call an ambulance?

I try to nod, but my head just rolls around.

—Don't want to see him get in trouble over being stupid. I'll make sure he's okay. If he don't get better, I'll take him to the hospital.

—He's lucky to have a friend like you. Bet he doesn't even apologize for fuckin' up your night.

I try to ask for help, but what comes out makes no sense.

—Okay, asshole, someone says. Whatever you say.

When I regain consciousness, I'm face down in the backseat of a dark car, my hands cuffed behind me.

The car is moving very slowly, and I can hear the loud, fat sound of motorcycles all around us. We must not have gone very far.

I twist around to see that the man who drugged me is driving.

When I try to sit up, I feel dizzy and sick.

—Guess I didn't give your ass enough junk, did I? Bitch dose was all I had.

I start to say something, but stop, not sure what there is to say.

—Bet you wish you'd've followed my friendly advice and left things the fuck alone.

—Why Casey? I ask.

—The fuck is Casey? She junkie bitch or replacement bitch? First fuckin' offed herself so we had to find another.

—Where is she?

—Chatty motherfucker all of a sudden, aren't you?

I can tell the effects of the drug are wearing off, but instead of trying to sit up, I remain still, moan occasionally, and continue to slur my speech.

—She's long gone, he says finally. Somewhere far away getting her little pink pussy and asshole fucked but good.

It's hard not to, but I don't say anything.

—She won't be coming back, he says. Just like you.

We're quiet a moment, the car starting and stopping every few feet.

—Can't *believe* that first bitch died on us. Thought Mr. Grantham was going to pop an aneurism or fuckin' stroke out or some shit. But when he see the other girl, he like her even better.

—How … I begin, trying to sound weak and out of it, were you … onto me so fast?

—This ain't no small-time operation, he says. Had someone watching the booth. Some other technical motherfucker hacked into the Thunder Beach phone lines, emails, computers and shit. The money these cats have …

I try to process what he's saying, integrate it with what I already know. My guess is the guy who called me first is with these guys, but the woman who called later is part of the official Thunder Beach event. She would've had no idea about the threats this guy made or the call from the other one.

The guy's ringtone goes off, and he answers his phone.

—Yeah?

Pause.

—The fuck you think I'm doin'?

Pause.

—Traffic's a bitch.

Pause.

—Bury him in the desert.

Pause.

—Motherfucker, it's an expression.

Pause.

—He ain't no cop.

Pause.

—I don't know, but—

He turns and looks at me, holding his phone away from his mouth.

—What's your story?

Turning back toward the front, he brings the phone back to his face.

—He's too fucked up to say shit.

Pause.

—Oh, he's working alone.

Pause.

—No … Probably personal. It's not a problem. We'll know soon enough. Where we meetin'?

Pause.

—We still pullin' out tonight?

Pause.

—Bitch, I'm asking what the boss said.

As he talks, I bring my foot up, place it beneath the door handle, and pull. As I suspected, it's locked, which is going to make this a little more tricky.

—I'll find out everything, he's saying. Won't take long.

The traffic causes him to have to stop again. When it does, I jump up, crouch in the seat, my back to the right side door. Bringing my cuffed hands up, I pull the lock up. Dropping down, I pull the handle, open the door, then I'm falling out backwards onto the pavement, tumbling onto the sand and oyster shell parking lot.

Rolling.

Twisting.

Standing.

Running.

Not sure where I am, I race down a small alley created by a T-shirt shop and a tattoo joint. Beyond the buildings, it's dark, but in the distance I see the lights of houses across a couple of vacant lots.

Behind me, I hear the car screech out of the traffic and into the parking lot, the bits of rock and shell crunching beneath the tires.

Lightheaded.

Weak.

Slow.

I'm running as fast as I can, but making very little progress.

Horns begin to honk.

People yell.

—Somebody call Nine-one-one, someone says.

—It's okay. I'm a cop, the big guy yells.

I glance back to see that he's now got a blue flashing light on his dashboard.

My feet get tangled up, and I fall hard. Unable to catch myself with my hands, I try to tuck under and take the brunt of the blow on my shoulder, but don't do it quite fast enough. The side of my head hits the ground hard.

I try to scramble to my feet, but he's there grabbing my arm, yanking me up.

As he pushes me back toward the car, he holds up a badge.

—Looks real, I say.

—Cop I took it off of was, he says. I'm gonna fuck you up a little extra just for the aggravation.

As we near the car, he stumbles on a piece of asphalt that had come off the street, and I sling my arm out of his grip. Lowering my shoulder, I lunge into him, and he goes down.

Running toward the road, I find the first biker who's by himself.

—I need help, I yell. Guy's not a cop. I swear. You can take me to the first cop you see.

—Hop on, he says.

He's a tall, thin older man with a long gray goatee and a ponytail coming out of a red bandana, do rag. The goatee reaches down below his chest, his ponytail halfway down his back.

—Guy's really not a cop, I say.

—Don't give a fuck if he is.

—He's trying to kill me, I say. He's part of a group who abducted a young girl. You can take me to a real cop if you don't—

—Hang on.

The big guy is up now, running toward us.

The traffic is not moving.

He's gonna get me again, I think, but the biker turns and speeds down the shoulder on the wrong side of the road in the direction we had just come from.

Holding on the best I can to the sissy bar with my cuffed hands, it feels like I could bounce off at any minute, and it reminds me of something I overheard about riding bitch. It was just a random snatch of conversation, two guys talking about how they'd never wrap their arms around the waist of another dude—even if their life depended on it. There's a reason there's nothing back there, one of them had said. When your bitch is riding bitch you want her holdin' on to you.

When I look back, the big guy is getting in his car. With the traffic, there's no way he'll catch up to us.

The biker dodges pedestrians and receives verbal abuse for a mile or so before getting back on the road.

—Where you wanna go?

—My car's at La Vela, I say, but you can drop me anywhere. Thank you so much. You saved my life—and that's not hyperbole.

—Not what?

—No exaggeration.

Back in the parking lot of La Vela, I look for someone who can take the cuffs off. The best I can do is a vendor booth that sells tires, windshields, and wheels that has a set of bolt cutters. I explain the situation, but the guy who does it for me doesn't seem to care.

With my hands untethered, I pull out Kevin's phone to call Rashard and Frank Clemmons, the bracelets sliding up and down my wrists as I do.

When I move my finger across the screen to unlock it, I see that Casey's phone is showing up again—and she's here at La Vela.

My quickening pulse pushes relief and excitement through me like a good drug, and I feel near euphoria.

Racing through the crowd, I follow the signal inside the club, up the incline to the left and to the information desk.

—Can I help you? the twenty-something brunette with a dark tan yells above the Metallica music.

—I'm looking for my daughter, I say, holding up Kevin's phone. My Family Map app says she's here.

—Huh?

I explain.

—I found an iPhone in the parking lot, she says. I just turned it on to try and call the owner.

—Let me see it.

—Call the number to let me know it's the right phone.

—You have more than one? I ask. Mine fell out of my pocket in the mens restroom in the Thunderdome.

—Who's that one belong to?

—My son.

—I tap in Casey's number and a sweet, romantic ringtone begins to play.

She hands me the phone.

—Where exactly did you find it?

—I can show you. What about your phone? Call it and I'll give it to you.

—I key in my number, my phone beeps, and she hands it to me.

—Come on.

She leads me out of the club and into the parking lot to a vacant spot between two tractor trailers with colorful murals on the sides—one for leather apparel and saddlebags, the other for performance parts.

—Right here, she says.

—Between these two—I begin, but then it hits me.

I remember what was parked here. I saw it last night. Pure Pleasure Massage and Escort Services.

She's nodding, when I become aware of her again.

—The trailer that was here, Pure Pleasure, when did it leave?

—I'm not sure, she says. Hasn't been very long ago.

—I think she's on a truck, I say. In a tractor trailer. Says Pure Pleasure on the side.

—What? Frank Clemmons asks. What makes you—

I give him a quick rundown of what I know and what I think.

—How sure are you?

—It's just a best guess, I say, but the guy acted like they're a big operation. I figure they're trafficking girls. Case is probably just one of many—chosen specifically for this Grantham guy.

—I'd hate to have every one of our guys looking for this truck and her not be on it.

I spot Gerry standing in front of the booth for the Bitches Pro Shop and have an idea.

—Then don't, I say. Put it out there and use some of your resources, and I'll get some extra help.

—How're you gonna—he begins, but I end the call and head over to a booth across the lot.

The Bitches Pro Shop is an all female motorcycle club that works to raise awareness about and resources for womens' issues, particularly domestic violence. I had featured Gerry and her girls in a piece I wrote on violence against women about a year ago.

This girl power group, in which nobody rides bitch, is perfect for helping find Casey.

—Hey Merrick, Gerry says as I walk up. You a rider now?

—Hey Gerry. I need your help.

—Name it.

As fast as I can, I tell her what's going on and what I need.

—So you just need us to locate the truck?

—As quickly as possible, I say. Do you guys have a way to communicate with each other?

—Radios and cell phones.

—Have them call nine-one-one when they spot it. Give them the location and tell them to let Detective Frank Clemmons of PCPD know immediately.

—Can do, she says. We'll split up, spread out, and run his ass aground.

As Gerry begins to gather her troops, I turn to scan the crowd, wondering if the big guy is going to show back up, and see Rashard walking toward me.

—Got your message, he says. What the hell's going on?

I tell him.

—*Fu-uck*, he says, holding it out.

—You gotta a handcuff key? I ask, holding up my wrists.

He pulls one out and takes off my bracelets.

—What's the word on Vic? I ask.

—Got an undercover set up on his house. We'll have him when

he goes home tonight—if not before.

—He started all this.

—We'll get 'im.

I nod, and began to look around.

—Whatta you about to do? he asks.

—Call in a few favors and start looking for the truck. You?

—Look around here a little bit. Talk to the manager—see what they know about the guys who rented the lounge for their little private party last night.

—Good idea.

—After all that's happened, he says, I want you take a couple of my friends with you when you go out looking for the truck.

—Sure. Who?

—Smith and Wesson.

Back in my car, this time with Rashard's friends, I try to figure out the best way to go. There was nothing in the man's phone conversation that let me know which direction they were headed. But he did say he was going to meet them, didn't he? He was headed west. Is that what they're doing?

There are only a few ways out of Panama City Beach—all highways, no interstates. If they *are* going west, they could be picking up I-10 in Pensacola, but they could just as easily be heading up 79, north through Ebro, or back through Panama City, picking up 231 to Dothan or 20 to Tallahassee.

I call Gerry.

—Are your riders concentrated in one area more than others?

—Most of them are out here around the beach, but some are up at the Outpost in Freeport or at Granny's in Wewa. All over. The ones here I'm sending out in every direction.

—Good.

—But with the way traffic is, I don't think they will have gotten very far.

—True. Thanks.

When she's gone, I think about what she said. She's right. There's no way the truck has made it very far at all. Chances are, they're trapped out here.

With an event like Thunder Beach on top of how congested PCB usually is, they had to know this could happen.

Do they even know we're aware of them? They could be just continuing their operation at a different location. But if they do know we're onto them, what will they do?

They seem too organized and well funded not to have a plan for just such a situation. What would it be? What are their options?

Easy—if you can't run, you have to hide.

Where and how can they hide?

The where is among other semis—like a truck stop, but there's not one anywhere on the beach. They were at the best place to hide—next to other Thunder Beach trailers. That's it. What if they just moved to a different Thunder Beach venue? The Boardwalk or Frank Brown Park or Edgewater.

I pull onto Thomas Drive and head toward Boardwalk.

I have an idea about how to get most of the people in the area looking for the truck, but wonder if going public might endanger Casey even more. If they don't know we're onto them, we'd be tipping them off, but we'll probably find them much, much quicker this way. Eventually, I conclude that involving more people is the way to go. It's a risk, but we've got to find her fast. I'm afraid if they get her out of town, we'll never see her again.

Withdrawing my phone, I call Emily Balazs, the news director of the local NPR affiliate WKGC.

When she answers, I explain the situation to her, give her Frank Clemmons as a contact for verification, and ask her to go on the air with a plea for help in finding Casey or locating the Pure Pleasure truck.

Emily agrees to help. Not only will she have an announcement on the air within minutes, but she'll contact the other radio stations in the area and ask them to run it as well.

Next, I call the two TV news stations, reaching Donna Bell at WJHG and Amy Hoyt at WMBB. As with Emily, I had worked with the two women on investigative reports over the years, and they agree to go on the air to make a plea for help finding the Pure Pleasure truck.

I then make one final call to Tony Simmons at *The News Herald*, who agrees to post the information on the paper's website and print it in tomorrow's edition.

At Boardwalk, I run toward the parked tractor trailers and begin to look around.

The approaching storm is much closer now, thunder rolling right off shore, lightning scribbling across the dark night sky, and I wonder how much longer the people will stay outside.

As I near the trucks and trailers, I see that some vendors are already beginning to pack up their products.

The atmosphere is electric, wind snapping vendor tent flaps and whirling bits of trash around. It won't be long now.

Like the trailers at the other rally locations, the ones lined up here are elaborately and intricately decorated, their sides enormous canvases for artistic advertisements of mostly motorcycle related gear.

Even in the darkening night, even from a distance, I can tell the Pure Pleasure trailer isn't among the twelve or so parked here, but I move closer to make absolutely certain.

My phone vibrates in my pocket, and I pull it out to see that it's Gerry.

—One of our girls thinks she's spotted it, she says.

—Where?

—West end of the beach. Almost to Pinnacle Port.

—That's great. Good work.

—She's moving in to get a closer look now. I'm not far from her, so I'm gonna head that way.

—Have you called Detective Clemmons?

—Waiting for confirmation before I do.

—Is it moving or—

—Yeah. Headed west on Back Beach.

—Let me know, I say and end the call.

I was wrong, I think. Not hiding. Running.

I walk back to my car, thrilled the truck has been found and disappointed I'm not there.

When I'm behind the wheel, the first smattering of raindrops pelt the windshield. Turning on the wipers, I smear them off.

The radio comes on and I hear Emily's impassioned voice.

Local police are asking for your help locating a Panama City girl who is believed to be in danger. Sources close to the case identify the girl as Casey Saunders, who is five foot five inches tall, with short blonde hair and green eyes. It's believed that Saunders' abduction may be related to a suspicious death of a woman whose body was discovered in the Marie

Motel Friday night.

Investigators believe Saunders is being held in the back of a trailer last seen in the La Vela parking lot. The trailer has logos that read Pure Pleasure Massage and Escort Services, and is believed to be here for the Thunder Beach weekend.

Again, authorities believe the abducted Casey Saunders is in extreme danger. If you have any information on the location of Casey or have seen the Pure Pleasure Massage and Escort Services trailer, you're urged to call 911 and ask for detective Frank Clemmons.

As I begin backing out, my phone vibrates again.

—Where are you? Rashard asks.

—Leaving Boardwalk.

—Waitress working the Posh Ultralounge for the private party last night said the man paying the bills is staying in a suite at Sterling Reef.

—That a condo?

—Yeah.

—Which one?

—On Front Beach right across from Miracle Strip. Said he kept bragging about his martinique sunset room, trying to get her to join him.

—Grantham?

—Yeah.

—She got a room number?

—Yeah. I told you, he wanted her to come over.

—What is it?

—I'm about to head over there, he says. You can meet me if you promise to—

—What's the goddamn room number? Casey could be in there. If I get there first, no way I'm waiting to go in.

I reach Sterling Reef before Rashard—by how much I'm not sure—but know he can't be far behind me.

It's raining now, steady, but the thunder and lightning, though much closer, are still out in the Gulf.

Parking in Alvin's Island's lot near the giant shark of Shipwreck Golf, I cross through the motorcycles on Front Beach in the cold rain, into the plush condo lobby, and up to Grantham's room, my two new best friends in my pocket.

In the elevator, my phone vibrates, and as I pull it out I see that it has very little charge left.

—Oh God, Merrick, Gerry says. This is so …

—What?

—These sick fucks. They actually have sex slaves in this truck. It's … I've never seen anything like it. I've—

—Is Casey there? Have you seen her? Is she okay?

—Let me check, she says. Let me just walk around and see if …

Actual slaves. Some are foreign, but some are young American girls. Very young. It's just … I'm having a hard time not throwing up or running past the police and pummeling one of these pricks. I'm so glad we're here, though. Several of the members of our club are helping the girls. Talking to them. Calming them down. Liz Jameson just got here. She's taking care of—

—That's great, but what about Casey? Did you find her? Can I speak to her?

—One more second. I've passed her picture out. I'm trying to find her now.

—How many are there?

—Eight.

It sounds like she covers the phone with her hand, her voice muffled and I can't make it out. She's gone for a minute or more.

As the elevator continues to rise, my stomach begins to sink, and a sense of dread descends on me.

—What is it? I ask.

No response.

—Gerry. What's wrong?

—Merrick, she's not here.

Before Gerry's call, I was actually thinking about waiting for Rashard outside Grantham's door, but with the increased likelihood Casey's on the other side, I have to go through it.

My plan is to knock on the door, say I have a message for Mr. Grantham, then turn so all he can see out of the peephole is the back of my head, but when I reach his room, I discover I have no need to do anything but walk in.

The door is kept open by the loop end of the door guard lock.

I suspect this means he's gone, but pull out the small revolver Rashard gave me, and slowly push open the door.

It's been a while since I've held a gun, and I've never done so in a situation like this. The last time I shot was at the range with my dad about three months ago.

The room is dark and cold and smells faintly of cigarette smoke and industrial air freshener.

Holding the gun with one hand while feeling for a light switch with the other, the wet copper smell reaches my nostrils just before I locate the lights and turn them on.

A lamp on a table in the foyer comes on, and reveals the large man who had drugged me earlier in the evening. He's lying on the floor on his side, his clothes and the area around him soaked in blood.

I can't be sure he's dead, but he doesn't appear to be breathing and there's so much blood, I don't really see how he couldn't be.

Carefully stepping around him, I venture deeper into the condo, bumping into nice furniture and feeling for light switches as I do.

The décor looks like something out of a discount catalog—the work of a busy interior designer—nice, but not too nice. Shades of cream, peach, and sea foam green. Definitely intended for a rental.

In the hallway, in the doorway of the bedroom, I find a large, older man lying face down in what looks to be more blood than one body can hold—shot to death like the first guy.

I assume it's Grantham, and a moment later the wallet on the bedroom dresser confirms my assumption.

Where is Casey?

I search through the rest of the condo wondering where Casey could be and who killed the two men.

I haven't gotten far when Rashard rushes in, gun drawn.

—What the fuck have you done? he says.

—They were like that when I got here. Swear. But I *am* wondering who saved us the trouble.

—Casey?

—Not here.

—No, I mean, could she have …

I shake my head.

—Can't imagine.

—Where is she? he asks.

—She wasn't on the truck. God, I hope we don't find her … If I don't get to her in time …

—Let's finish searching the place, then we'll get crime scene in here and see what they can tell us.

Time passes.

Then some more.

Then some more.

I pull my phone out to see what time it is, but it's dead.

I'm sitting on the floor in the hallway outside of the condo trying to figure out what I missed when Frank Clemmons comes out.

—I recognize that look, he says.

—Yeah? I say, pushing myself up.

—Don't do it. You did everything you could—far more than anybody else. These things never have a happy ending.

I nod.

Crime scene techs in white suits, shoe covers, and latex gloves come in and out of the unit carrying various instruments and evidence bags.

I'm so tired, so spent, I find it difficult to hold my head up—and it's not just fatigue, but defeat, all the tension I've been carrying around now dissipated, the adrenaline levels plummeted.

—Any evidence she was here? I ask.

—Somebody else was—female, blonde, probably her. Won't know for sure until … for a while.

—Any idea what happened in there?

He shakes his head.

—Somebody shot them with a small caliber handgun, probably a .38, but beyond that …

When the techs had first arrived, they had, with Clemmons' apologies, examined my gun and tested my hands for GSR.

—How long they been dead? I ask.

—Not long. Don't know for sure, but—

—Could it've been the guy from Jade Gardens?

—He's still in custody.

I nod and think about it some more.

—Why don't you go home? he says. Get some rest. I'll let you know if we turn up anything. I swear I will.

I walk to my car in a hard, slanting rain.

My clothes and hair are soaked through in seconds, but I hardly notice and don't care.

Lightning pops all around me, thunder rumbling angrily in the dark night sky, the long-awaited storm finally unleashing its fury on Front Beach.

The same questions keep rolling around my mind—Where is Casey? What happened to her? Who killed Grantham and the other man? If not the man from Jade's, then—

As lightning strikes a nearby transformer and the lights for several blocks go out, I realize who it is—who it has to be.

Vic Dyson.

Has to be.

Wonder if his plan all along was to put them on to her so they'd snatch her and he could take her from them. Or maybe the deal was he'd get her once Grantham was done.

Dodging drenched motorcyclists, I run to my car, and am about to get in, when I see his van parked in the back of Alvin's, where it had been earlier in the week.

I run over and look inside.

No one's up front, and I can't see in the back.

With the butt of Rashard's gun, I break the passenger side window and unlock the door.

Among the paint and supplies in the back, there are certain tools and materials that could be part of a rape kit, but no Casey, no Vic.

Running around the dark, mostly empty lot looking for them, the intermittent lightning illuminating the wet world below, I wipe raindrops from my eyes in an attempt to see.

Where can he be? Why is he out here again?

As I run back toward my car, lightning flashes across the way, exposing the old, abandoned buildings of Miracle Strip, and I think he could be hiding there.

When, between the strikes, I see the beam of a flashlight from within the park, I know it.

In the time it takes for the thought to form and finish, I'm racing across the street in a dead run.

Growing up in the area, coming to Miracle Strip Amusement Park was a huge part of my childhood summers. I'd come several times a season—with parents, grandparents, friends, youth groups—and have far more fun than at any of the much larger theme parks in Central Florida.

I was here on its final weekend, to mourn its loss, when, after forty-one years of continuous operation and over twenty million visitors, Miracle Strip was no more, and like other locals, the only thing that bothers me more than its closing is the way what's left of it has sat languishing as the planned condos meant to go up in its place were abandoned just like the park is now.

Jumping over a fallen sawhorse roadblock, I run through the overgrown parking lot toward the giant oblong, red and yellow ENTRANCE sign with the empty blue flag poles behind it, lightning strikes exposing the weeds, bushes, and debris littering the wet asphalt.

Overhead, palm trees lining the entrance path sway in the strong wind, its force turning the raindrops into pellets.

The property is protected by a chain link fence, which won't be difficult to climb, but not wanting to do it in the open, I veer to the left, past what's left of the bumper cars—a square platform with a rusting sheet metal floor—and over behind the building where live musical shows were performed.

Making my way further down, I climb over a double gate near the old Log Flume, tearing my jeans and cutting a gash in my leg on a piece of rusted barbed wire.

The ride is now gone, but the cement riverbed and foundation supports are still in place. Too wide to jump, I have to wade across twelve feet of water that comes up about halfway on my shin. Now my tennis shoes are soaked through, sloshing as I make my way to the wooden structure that served as the entrance and exit of the ride.

The structure is so overgrown it looks like I've just discovered it in the middle of the deep woods. Jumping over the metal crowd dividers, I pass beneath where the giant paddlewheel used to be, and tromp through the spot where the cars from Route 63, the train, and the Log Flume would, at certain magical moments, intersect.

The water here is wider, and as I navigate through it, I trip over a fallen plank, landing face first in the shallow water.

Climbing up the sloping concrete, I pass overgrown gazebos and random stacks of discarded lumber, pausing for a moment next to the small Mexican Cantina building to look for the flashlight beam again.

Vandals have broken all the windows of the tile and mason concession stand, and in purple spray paint written SATAN EATS HERE.

All rides removed, all that remains of the once thriving amusement park is a dozen or so mostly empty buildings. Some of the rides appear to be present because their buildings, so identified with them, still stand—the old spooky structure of The Haunted Castle, the green monster of The Abominable Snowman, the red devil of Dante's Inferno—but they are just shells, gutted of the amusement they used to house. Colorful facades, grave markers of the bygone era of my youth.

I don't see the flashlight beam, but in the darkness and driving rain it's hard to see anything, and in the over-illumination of the lightning flashes there's too much to take in.

Deciding to make a sweep of the park, I continue past a vine covered bathroom building with a huge pile of boards and blocks and large chunks of asphalt in front of it.

Beyond a broken bench and severely leaning oak tree, I come up between the entrances to Route 63, the small track car ride, and the giant igloo fronted by the monster of the Abominable Snowman.

Cars and track gone, the open red, white, and blue structure of Route 63 is graffiti-covered, its galvanized crowd dividers leaning and in some cases fallen, all that's left of its sign part of an American flag and the word ROUTE.

To my right, the entrance to the igloo that is the building of the Abominable Snowman ride is in between the legs of an enormous green gorilla-looking creature that stands some thirty feet in the air. The ride long since removed, the igloo is a large, round all black room with a high ceiling.

Pulling out Rashard's gun, I enter slowly, my back to the left wall, scraping my shoulder on a piece of exposed rebar as I do.

Darkness.

The blacker-than-black building is like a cave. I can't see anything. He could be right next to me and I—

Lightning flashes and he's there.

Standing across the room, pointing a gun at me.

Without hesitation, I squeeze the trigger of my gun, the explosion deafening as it bounces around the echo chamber of the enclosure.

Dropping and rolling away, I wait.

There is only the sound of rain, the rumble of thunder.

When the lightning flashes again, I can see what I thought was Vic—my reflection in a funhouse type wall mirror across the way.

I had shot myself—or my reflection—not something to bolster confidence.

I'm shocked at how easily I fired the gun, and more than a little disturbed, but don't have time to think about it now.

Ears ringing, I run back out into the rain, realizing firing the round so foolishly had alerted him to my presence. If it's even him. It could be a vandal, a graffiti artist, or a homeless person.

So stupid. I could've killed Casey or some kid here to explore what's left of the park. Get it together. Take a breath. Slow down. Be careful.

On the chance it's him, on the slightest possibility that he has Casey here, I could use some help searching the place. Pulling out my phone to call Rashard, I turn it back on, hoping it has enough charge left for one call, but it doesn't even power up.

I regretted stowing Kevin and Casey's phones away in the console of my car for safe keeping. I couldn't have carried three phones, and I needed the numbers programmed in mine, but I now wish I had checked to see which had the most charge. Of course, I couldn't have predicted my current predicament.

Ducking out of the rain into the open Boardwalk Fries and musical show building, I see an old tractor trailer and the only two remaining rides in the park—the biplanes and hot air balloons, which have been disassembled and are being stored here. One of the biplanes has been pulled up to the front, as if some kids intended to take it, only to discover it was too heavy.

I search the building as fast as I can, and head back out into the park, stumbling over a fire extinguisher as I do. Catching myself, attempting to keep moving without falling, a shot rings out of the storm, a muzzle flash from across the way, as a round whizzes by me and shatters the side of one of the small plastic hot air balloons.

Running toward the flash, hiding behind trees and the corner of buildings as I do, I quickly scan the area every time the lightning strikes, but the shooter isn't visible.

Climbing through the railing, I cross over the Route 63 entrance, past the depot near the large rusting train wheels, and come out near the service road on the back side of the park beside a dilapidated greenhouse, now mostly a wooden skeleton with strips of opaque plastic flapping in the storm.

Nearby, rusting refrigerators, washing machines, hot water heaters, and lawn mowers spill out of a tin shed way too small to hold the discarded appliances.

The woods, through which the train used to run, are thick back here, and I have to decide if I should search them or head back into the park.

Regardless of where Vic is, it's more likely he has Casey in one of the buildings of the park—can't take her home to mother's trailer—so I run down the service road, coming out beside the wooden tracks of the Starliner rollercoaster, the park's first and best ride. When it was taken apart and sold to Cypress Gardens, the only thing that couldn't be reused were the red planks and support joints, and so all that is left of the best ride to ever grace Panama City Beach is a huge stack of wooden track.

Passing it, I actually hear echoes of screaming riders, the click and clack of chain and track, and the roar and screech of wheels on rails.

Running into the large square opening where the ride was removed from Dante's Inferno, I scan the round, black shell. Tiny lights still hang from the ceiling, air conditioning duct still runs along the back wall, part of a plywood platform for stepping up onto and off of the ride remains, but there's nothing else.

Racing down the stairs, out of the throat, through the mouth and onto the tongue of the red devil, I pause on the wet pavement and look around.

Lightning flashes and the thirty-foot high devil head with triangular pupils, arched eyebrows, pointed ears, and a thin black, pencil mustache glows brightly behind me.

The sound of the shot is lost in the thunder, but I hear the *thwack* of the bullet as it splinters one of Dante's teeth hanging above me.

Vic fires again, and this time I see the muzzle flash from the porch of The Haunted Castle.

I fire a round back and run toward him.

The Haunted Castle was an old-fashioned, two-seater car ride that bumped around a track as Day-Glo horrors appeared, then whipping the next corner would use flashing lights and loud noises to reveal automated monsters in chicken wire cages.

In the darkness, the huge, snarling skull with the oozing black sockets still glows spookily beneath the porch of the abandoned castle.

As I pass the eerie green glow of the rotating tunnel, Vic fires a round from inside and it hits me in the upper arm.

Dropping the revolver, I fall to the ground, searing pain shooting out of my shoulder.

I can't see him, but I hear his footsteps running toward me from inside the tunnel, shooting at me as he comes.

Rounds splinter the wood floor near me as I reach for the gun.

Pain explodes in my thigh.

He's gotten me again.

And then I hear it.

It's one of the best sounds I've ever heard.

Click.

Click.

Click.

Dry fires as he continues to pull the trigger of an empty revolver.

Grabbing the gun with my left hand, I roll over in excruciating pain and fire the rest of the rounds at him.

I have no idea how many times I hit him, but it's enough to knock him down.

He falls just a few feet away from me.

I crawl over to him, grab his shoulders and shake him.

—Where is she?

He doesn't respond.

There's a lot of blood. Some of it's mine, but much more of it is his.

I notice for the first time, three holes in his midsection, one of them very close to his heart.

—Where's Casey?

He mumbles something, but I can't make it out.

—What?

He tries to say something, but this time nothing comes out.

—Tell me, I yell. Where is she? Don't die with this on your conscience. Don't. Tell me now. Where is she?

He lifts his hand and I think he's going to try to hit me, but he points toward the small, flattop green building of the original offices that used to be beneath the Starliner.

I run the length of the arcade building, the far end still bearing the purple letters of the RISING STAR STUDIO sign.

The little office building, like every other one left in the abandoned property, is overgrown and in disrepair—glass broken, walls filled with graffiti.

Only a jagged piece of hanging glass is left in the front door. I duck beneath it, as lightning illuminates Casey's vulnerable little body on a dirty quilt spread out on the floor.

—Casey?

I say her name gently, my voice low and soft.

She is bound and gagged and semiconscious.

When she opens her eyes and attempts a weak smile up at me, I begin to weep, and I can't remember ever being as happy or relieved in my entire life.

As carefully as I can, I remove her gag and begin to untie her.

—Are you okay? I ask.

She shakes her head.

—But, she says, I will be.

—Yes, you will, I say. You most certainly will. But, sorry, that was a stupid question. I meant are you hurt.

—Not too bad. Where's—she begins, looking around, searching

the darkness for monsters.

—Dead. They're all dead. Grantham. Vic. Everyone who hurt you is dead or in custody.

—You're bleeding, she says. Are you okay?

—I've never been better. Not ever.

The storm over, we limp out of what's left of Miracle Strip in the breaking day, leaning on each other.

The morning is clean and calm, the air fresh, and I know it's going to be a good day.

From the parking lot, I flag down a cop coming from Grantham's crime scene at the Sterling Reef, and in moments both Rashard and Clemmons are helping us into an ambulance.

They send two, but we insist on riding together.

—Missy, Frank says to Casey, it's no exaggeration to say that this man saved your life. He's been ahead of everyone every step of the way.

She nods.

—I knew he'd come for me.

—He came like a son of a bitch, Rashard says.

—No dad would do any less for his daughter, I say.

She lays her head on my good shoulder and I rest my head on hers.

Two days later, I receive a two word text from Regan that reads: I'm sorry.

I think a long time about what to say, not wanting to repeat the same cycle with her again.

I'm hurt and trying to work through it. I don't want to respond in anger. If possible, I'd like to end things amicably, but for a long while I don't know exactly how to reply.

Though there is something almost pathological about her back-and-forth behavior, I honestly don't think there's anything malicious in her. Her attraction and desire for me, her every kindness—all seemed authentic. Still do. Even her telling me she loved me—I truly believe she meant it at the time.

Eventually, I realize what I must do and then I know what I should say.

To her two words, I reply with three of my own—the final three I ever communicate to her.

I forgive you.

By Thursday of the following week, Casey and Kevin are moving in with me in my little clapboard house on the banks of the Apalachicola River.

Casey and I are healing, and we're both seeing a counselor. She's severely damaged from her horrific experience, but every day she gets a little better, a little stronger, a little more like the Casey before the monsters got her. John Milton stops by often to check on us, and has his deputies routinely patrol our neighborhood, and I can tell Casey finds it extremely reassuring.

For my part, I am already beginning to imagine an existence without guilt and self-punishment. Having Casey and Kevin in my life again makes this possible.

In my interaction with these two amazing people, we feel like what we are—family.

—Hey Merrick. Hey Merrick. Do you have high-speed internet? Kevin asks as we carry boxes up the steps and onto the porch. I need high-speed internet. I really need it.

—We've got it, I say.

—*Coo-ool.*

I've accepted the position with the online news startup, and, for the moment, have money in my pocket. My first feature is on sex trafficking, and Casey and I are working with Liz Jameson to eradicate it—starting with Panama City, but not stopping until it no longer exists anywhere in the world.

—Do you have—do you have a—a wireless router? Kevin asks. A wireless router and the premium movie channel Home Box Office in high definition and a—a high definition television to-to watch it on?

—Yes we do, I say.

—*Coo-ool,* he says, placing his box on the porch table and dancing around. Did you hear that, Casey?

—I did, she says.

—What do you think about —about—about that?

—I think we have everything we need, she says.

—We do, I say. Everything we need in the whole wide world.

Michael Lister is an award-winning novelist, essayist, screenwriter, and playwright who lives in North Florida. A former prison chaplain, Michael is the author of the "Blood" series featuring prison chaplain/detective, John Jordan (*Blood of the Lamb*, *The Body and the Blood*, etc.). His second series features Jimmy "Soldier" Riley, a PI in Panama City during World War II (www.FloridaNoir.com). Michael's recent literary thrillers include *Double Exposure*, *Thunder Beach*, and *Burnt Offerings*. In addition to fiction, Michael writes a weekly column on art and meaning titled Of Font and Film (www.OfFontandFilm.com), which includes reviews of film and fiction. When Michael isn't writing, he teaches college, and operates a charity and community theater. His website is www.MichaelLister.com